BEIJING
SPRAWL

BEIJING SPRAWL

XU ZECHEN

TRANSLATED FROM CHINESE BY
**JEREMY TIANG
& ERIC ABRAHAMSEN**

TWO LINES
PRESS

"Wheels Turn" first appeared under the title "Wheels are Round" in *Shi Cheng: Short Stories from Urban China* (Comma Press, 2013)
"The Dog's Been Barking All Day" first appeared in *Freeman's*
"Climbing Stork Tower" on pages 167–168 translated by Xu Yuanchong

ISBN 978-1-949641-32-5
Ebook ISBN 978-1-949641-33-2

Two Lines Press
582 Market Street, Suite 700, San Francisco, CA 94104
www.twolinespress.com

Typeset by Stephanie Nisbet
Printed in the United States of America

Library of Congress Cataloging-in-Publication Data
Names: Xu, Zechen, 1978- author. | Abrahamsen, Eric, translator. Tiang, Jeremy, translator.
Title: Beijing Sprawl by Xu Zechen ; translated by Eric Abrahamsen & Jeremy Tiang.
Other titles: Kan, zhe jiu shi Beijing. English
Description: San Francisco, CA : Two Lines Press, [2023] | Summary: "An exploration of the true meaning of 'home,' this short story collection comprises nine vignettes about the lives of four friends who share a small apartment on the outskirts of Beijing"-- Provided by publisher.
Identifiers: LCCN 2022054894 (print) | LCCN 2022054895 (ebook)
ISBN 9781949641325 (paperback) | ISBN 9781949641332 (ebook)
Subjects: LCSH: Xu, Zechen, 1978---Translations into English.
LCGFT: Urban fiction. | Short stories.
Classification: LCC PL2969.Z43 K3613 2023 (print) | LCC PL2969.Z43 (ebook)
DDC 895.13/6--dc23/eng/20230117
LC record available at https://lccn.loc.gov/2022054894
LC ebook record available at https://lccn.loc.gov/2022054895

1 3 5 7 9 10 8 6 4 2

This publication is supported in part by an award from the National Endowment for the Arts.

CONTENTS

SIX-EARED

MACAQUE

Six-Eared Macaque

"As I see the matter, the specious Wu-k'ung must be a six-eared macaque, for even if this monkey stands in one place, he can possess the knowledge of events a thousand miles away and whatever a man may say in that distance. That is why I describe him as a creature who has

A sensitive ear,
Discernment of fundamental principles,
Knowledge of past and future,
And comprehension of all things.

The one who has the same appearance and the same voice as the true Wu-k'ung is a six-eared macaque."

~Tathāgata Buddha in *Journey to the West*
by Wu Cheng'en (tr. Anthony C. Yu)

There was only one guy who jogged in full suit and tie early in the morning on 23rd Street, and that was my old friend Feng Nian. He hadn't been sleeping well for a while, waking with a bad dream in the middle of the night. He'd stare at the ceiling for two or three hours before dropping off again, and in the morning his brain would be mush. One morning, still groggy, he came knocking at my door, asking what to do. I've had weak nerves forever, and his symptoms were child's play to me. I had one word of advice for him: run. Or two words: go jogging. I couldn't speak to nightmares or insomnia, but when it came to dizziness and a fuzzy brain, I was quite the expert. Jogging cleared the mind. And so, every few days, Feng Nian joined me for a run through the alleyways on the western edge of Beijing. To get to work on time, he had to leave the house in full battle dress, and right after our jog he would cram himself onto the bus for his commute. Just imagine a narrow, twisting alley. Now picture a guy in a smart suit jogging down it. I thought it was weird, anyway. But there was no helping it. Feng Nian kept loosening his necktie and rubbing his throat. "How am I supposed to sleep, Muyu?" he'd say to me. "I wake up feeling like I've got a chain around my neck. I can't catch my breath."

His dream was weird as well. It was always the same one: that he'd turned into a six-eared macaque dressed in a suit and tie, his handler leading him out to perform. He'd go through a number of tricks: somersaults, cycling, jumping through a ring of fire, stilt-walking, juggling three tennis balls, horseback riding, and so on. Never mind that it was exhausting, the worst thing was that, after the show, his handler would fling him over one shoulder and walk off with him on his back. In the dream, he understood clearly that he was a six-eared macaque named Feng Nian, and around his neck was permanently fastened a gleaming silver chain... or maybe it was stainless steel. His entire body weight dangled from that collar, as he hung from his handler like a backpack. The chain dug into his fur, his skin, his flesh. He felt his throat constrict more and more, as if he were suffocating. He *was* suffocating. He couldn't breathe; his face was as red as his rump.

The dream was always the same, with minor variations: If he rode a bicycle one night, he'd juggle the next, or do two or three tricks at once. The other difference was that he found it increasingly hard to catch his breath when waking up. Which is to say, he came slightly closer to strangling each night. He'd feel the handler sling him over his shoulder by the chain, like a bundle or a sack, a little more violently each time, with a little more force, and thanks to gravity, the chain grew ever tighter. Feng Nian was certain that if he didn't wake up when he did, he'd surely stop breathing altogether.

I had two questions that Feng Nian couldn't answer. First, why would he keep having the same dream over and over? If you thought about it, there was progression, so these were actually installments of one long dream. Anyone with weak nerves knows we dream a lot, and sometimes a dream can recur, picking up where it left off, nothing new there, but such frequency, such unyielding repetition and development, seemed impossible for even a person with the weakest nerves—yet somehow Feng Nian had done it. My second question was about the six-eared macaque. I went to Haidian Library and looked it up: There's no such thing as a six-eared macaque. Even genetic mutation hadn't produced anything like a six-eared macaque, a creature that existed only in *Journey to the West*. I knew this one: In the book, the Monkey King meets another version of himself, identical inside and out, with exactly the same abilities—an adversary he can't defeat. Monkey was the Great Sage, the Equal of Heaven. Confronted with another Great Sage, he was at a loss. In the end, he defeated the false Monkey only with the help of the Tathāgata Buddha, who said, "This guy is a six-eared macaque." The six-eared macaque from the book actually had only two ears, as did the six-eared macaque in Feng Nian's dream. But the monkey in the dream named Feng Nian really was the six-eared macaque. He was very clear about this.

He dreamed that he was both Feng Nian and a monkey: There's already plenty to talk about there, even before getting to this monkey happening to be a non-existent six-eared macaque. You can't go that far afield, not even in a dream. The first few times he told us about his weird dream, we didn't think anything of it. He'd come round to our pingfang asking us to interpret the dream: Xingjian, Miluo, Baolai, and me. Baolai was twenty, the oldest; I was the youngest, having just turned seventeen. We didn't know jack shit about that sort of thing, so we made stuff up.

Xingjian said, "Isn't it obvious? You need a woman."

Miluo's interpretation was, "You don't earn enough money, but you want to be your own boss."

"Bullshit, I'm too busy to think about women," said Feng Nian. "And I've always made enough to get by, since I started working. Me, a boss? I should stand there bare-assed waiting to get kicked?"

Baolai's suggestion was a little more out of the box. "Feng, I think you're homesick."

This attracted a stream of mockery from Xingjian

and Miluo. Only a moron like Baolai would keep bringing up homesickness. "If you miss home so much, why did you leave? Might as well have stayed in Huajie village, working a crappy job and waiting to die."

Then it was my turn: "Feng, there's something wrong with your brain."

That got him worked up. "You bastard. What kind of talk is that?"

But I was just telling the truth. Weird dreams are the province of weak nerves, and what are those but a problem with your brain? Feng Nian waved my words away, telling me to be serious. I pursed my lips. Believe it or not, when it comes to weak nerves, I've always been completely serious.

*

Among the people from Huajie who lived in the neighborhood, Feng Nian tried the hardest to seem respectable. No one else went around in a suit all the time. I had lived a dozen courtyards over from him, back home in Huajie in Zhejiang Province. So I knew him really well, and as far as I was aware, he'd never once worn a suit back home. One year, there was a strange wave of fashion, and suddenly everyone was wearing suits: men and women, adults and kids. All the way from the stone pier to the paved road, you'd see these villagers in suits coming at you, which gave you the sense of being helplessly unmoored in time. I was away at boarding school then, and when I came back for vacation, I thought aliens had taken over. Feng Nian was one of the few people in normal clothes among all those aliens. Yet now, in the closet of his rented room, he had at least four cheap suits, plus some ties. He worked at an electronics shop in Zhongguancun, and his boss was very insistent that they had to show their customers respect in all ways. That meant suits for the men, and skirt-suits for the women that revealed their shapely calves even in the depths of winter.

Baolai and I headed to Peking University for some fun. On the way, we stopped by Hailong Electronics to see Feng Nian. Crushed by the crowd, I began to sweat. Feng Nian stood at the entrance in his suit, arms folded, perspiration beading on the tip of his nose, saying to each person as they entered, "Welcome, this way please, have a look and see which style of camera you like." His voice was growing hoarse. He gave his spiel to Baolai and me, and realized only afterward that it was us. I wandered around the shop. Sure enough, all the staff were in suits, like a bunch of brides and grooms. It was almost closing time, so Baolai said we'd wait for Feng Nian.

"No need," said Feng Nian. "We're closing late—pushing holiday sales."

"But don't you have to get off work eventually?"

"Get lost, you two, and don't let my manager see you." He was getting agitated. "We're not allowed to chit-chat during work hours."

"Fine, you go on standing there," I said.

"Except for lunch and pee breaks, I stand here all fucking day."

I don't know anything about fashion, but even I

could tell his suit was pretty much the worst in the entire shop, and his white shirt was drenched with sweat. So he stood all the more solemnly and was even more enthusiastic in greeting the gods who walked past him. As his boss liked to say, "If your hardware isn't great, make up for it with your software." Baolai constantly tightened his cheap, clip-on tie. The opposite of his endless loosening in the mornings as he ran.

I once asked him, as if I were one of those psychologists you see on TV, whether the over-tight ties had damaged his psyche, and that's why he kept dreaming of being strangled. He thought about it and said, "Ties *are* annoying, and when the bosses have nothing better to do, they inspect our necks, checking if the knots are tight enough, but it's going too far to say it scarred me or darkened my soul."

"Then why are you always pulling at your tie?"

"Because I can't stop thinking about the nightmare. I get confused, and it feels like this thing is that chain around my neck."

I had it backward, is what he was saying. He loosened his tie because of the dream, but the tie wasn't what caused the dream. Fine, then. That was the end of my psychiatric evaluation.

I visited his shop one other time, on a day I was ball-achingly bored. I'd gotten a bit of spending money from my uncle, Thirty Thou Hong, and felt like a real tycoon. Passing through Zhongguancun, I bought a couple of roasted yams and headed for Hailong. Feng Nian gave me a terrified look and refused to take one. Not only was he not allowed to eat on the job, he couldn't even have friends stop by. I got a bit annoyed.

Here I am, dude, dropping by to say hello with nothing but good intentions, and somehow I've offended you? But he kept trying to chase me out.

"Can't you pretend I'm a customer?"

"You?" said Feng Nian. "Man, take a look in the mirror and tell me what you think."

I glanced at the mirror, and sure, I didn't particularly look like a big spender, but who says rich people go around dripping with gold and diamonds all the time? I smoothed down my jacket and asked one of his co-workers, "Miss, excuse me, do you think I look respectable?"

She laughed and said, "Sure, quite respectable," in Tieling-accented Mandarin. So I gave her the roasted yam. Even this alarmed Feng Nian—his friend leaving physical evidence behind. "Dude, I'll buy you ten roast yams, how about that?" he said, his brows contorted in agony, his face sunk in despair. A few times after that, he mentioned treating me to roast yams, but I refused to let him.

If it had been up to me, I'd never have set foot in that shop again. That's something Xingjian always talked about: sticking to our guns. So I had stayed away, but now here I was again, at the shop entrance, yelling to Feng Nian, "Your ma wants you to call home now, right away, immediately, no excuses!"

That afternoon, I'd been jogging past Blossoms Bar and stopped to call home from the newsstand phone booth out front. My father didn't care if he heard from me, as long as I was still alive, but Ma had a rule: I had to let her know at least twice a month that I was all right. Even that little thing, those brief conversations, were irksome to me. I was about to hang up when Ma suddenly said, "Your Auntie Feng just came in; she wants a word with you."

Auntie Feng hollered at the phone from our front door, "Hey, kid, when is that son of mine getting home?"

"How would I know when he's getting home?"

"You don't know?" She was holding the receiver now, but shouting just as loudly as she had from the doorway. "He's supposed to come back here to meet a girl! Tell him to call his parents now, right away, immediately, no excuses. Old Man Zheng is waiting for an answer!"

When Ma had taken the phone back, I asked her, "Which Old Man Zheng?"

"How many are there? When you were a kid, you chased him for miles and miles. Zheng Mahe, the monkey handler."

"Oh. Well, Feng Nian's at work."

"So? He can call from work."

All right, then. It was 3:12 PM and I was going to break my boycott. If I waited till he got off work, Monkey Zheng's daughter might have fallen in love with someone else. I was jogging anyway, so I ran to Zhongguancun. Panting in the shop's doorway, I shouted to Feng Nian, "Your ma wants you to call home now, right away, immediately, no excuses!"

Then I turned and walked away. He called after me, but I ignored him. He could go suck eggs. Jogging home, I came to my senses. There had been no need to go charging into his shop to pass on the message—he couldn't be into Monkey Zheng's daughter; otherwise, he'd have bragged about her. Among a group of bachelors like us, nothing gave you more bragging rights than having a woman. Some made sure to let the crew know if they so much as saw a female pig. What's more, the bastard hadn't been honest with me. He'd said he had no idea why he kept turning into a six-eared macaque on a leash in his dreams. Surely he knew it was because he was scared of Monkey Zheng. But there was something I didn't understand. Monkey Zheng was on the rough side, and his face was nauseating from any angle, which is why everyone in Huajie called him that. So it made sense to be scared of him. But his daughter, Zheng Xiaohe, took after her mother. She was modest, demure, plump, and pale—not a great beauty, but still way out of Feng Nian's league. If I'd had to guess, I'd have said Feng Nian was overcome with delight, and that's why he kept having nightmares. They do say great joy leads to sorrow.

*

"Bullshit!" Feng Nian was watching us play Ace of Spades on our roof. "I was already a monkey for god knows how many nights before I found out about this."

So we had to assume he had special powers, like Huajie's blind fortune-teller—Half-Immortal Hu—who could predict major events within a two-year time frame. Good luck had been coming for him, and Feng Nian's subconscious had gotten excited in advance.

"Why do I have to come from the same village as

you degenerates? I don't know what the hell my ancestors were thinking."

"Don't talk like that, Nian." Xingjian said, putting down his cards. "We're not degenerates. Real talk…if Zheng Xiaohe isn't the woman for you, I'll put a bun in her oven in just a couple of dreams. Just a couple. Think about it, pale and round, plump and smooth, running your hands over her…"

Feng Nian's hand sliced through the air, cutting off Xingjian's daydream. "Enough of that," he said. "It's not that I don't like her, but that bastard Monkey Zheng is insisting I go back to Huajie."

"You should start calling him by his real name," I reminded him.

"Fine, that bastard Zheng Mahe. But what would I go back there for? To do monkey tricks with him?"

"Why not bring Zheng Xiaohe to Beijing?" Baolai suggested. "Get married, raise a bunch of kids."

"She doesn't want to come." Feng Nian stood and began pacing around our flat roof, brushing off his jacket. "She said, 'What would I do over there, dress you up in a suit? Knot your tie for you?' I didn't utter a word. How could I afford to support her? Then she said, 'If I live there, will I have to wear a suit and tie too?'"

"What did you say to that?" Miluo asked.

"Didn't so much as fart. There's no answer to something like that. Six years of crappy jobs, and this is all I've managed to make of myself?"

All our moods were ruined. The mere mention of crappy jobs was damaging to our self-esteem. We'd all hoped to make something of ourselves, but just look at us.

Zheng Xiaohe had a pretty good job in Huajie village. Her ba spent his life as a monkey handler, for decades traveling all over until he couldn't hack it any longer. Just as he and his monkey were settling into retirement, the government suddenly set up a scenic walkway along the riverside, and like a trickster Monkey Zheng transformed himself into a folk artist. With his old monkey, its rump dark with age, he became a fixture on the promenade, performing for tourists at scheduled times every day. As an additional bonus, Xiaohe got a job selling riverboat tickets. Given the low cost of living in Huajie, her wages went just as far as what Feng Nian was earning in Beijing. That's why she wasn't willing to relocate. It's not that she didn't want to, but she'd reached the age of marriage and childbearing, and women don't have time to waste—even if she did come, she'd have to go back sooner or later. It wasn't easy to find work in Huajie, and she couldn't afford to give up the opportunity she had; otherwise, she might end up falling between two stools.

We all expressed deep sympathy for Zheng Xiaohe's position. An even bigger problem was Monkey Zheng—he was adamant that Feng Nian return to the village. After a lifetime of drifting on the wind, he'd come to believe it was best for men to settle down at home. Feng Nian found this bizarre.

"I know," said Miluo. "He's afraid you'll pick up bad habits from the outside world."

"Bullshit," said Feng Nian. "When would I manage to pick up bad habits? I don't have the money to gamble, and even if I could afford to visit a prostitute,

I couldn't find the time. I stand in one place all day, talking my mouth dry—by the time I'm in bed, I've forgotten I'm a man. Then, all night long, I'm faced with that shiny silver chain. How would I get corrupted?"

I said, "Monkey Zheng doesn't know about your great, bitter suffering."

"I remember how Monkey Zheng used to be quite the playboy in his younger days." Xingjian flipped over his last card: the ace of spades. He'd won again. "He might look like shit, but he got laid all the time. I heard he got the clap, and now he has to spend half an hour every night in the bathtub dosing himself. Maybe he's afraid Feng Nian will fight him for the tub."

"Listen, motherfucker," said Feng Nian, "I'm thirty years old, and my junk is still in its original packaging."

We all burst out laughing at that. True enough, our Feng Nian was already thirty. If he'd stayed in Huajie, he'd have a child old enough to be sent to the store for soy sauce by now.

He was thirty, which was why Uncle and Auntie Feng were worried. Age was always a concern when it came to getting married. What was he waiting for? The longer he held off, the lower his market value. Feng Nian surely understood that better than any of us, which explained his anxiety. We talk about life as though it's finding the next stepping stone to get across a river, but the vast majority of people can actually see their whole lives laid out clearly. We just replicate what the generation before us did, and the generation before them, and so on. All our forebears lived like this, and we have no hope for some miracle. Feng Nian wouldn't be able to stay in Beijing forever. With his level of talent, ability, and luck, he'd surely end up just like ninety-five percent of people. He should take a few bites of life while young, then push the bowl aside and walk away. He was clinging to Beijing, but that was a young person's game. It was time to settle down—he needed a reminder that thirty was no longer young. Yet he still dressed himself up in a suit every day, trying to seem respectable—that's how I knew he wasn't ready to give up, even though there was no sign of his luck turning.

"Besides the manager and deputy manager," Feng Nian said sadly on our rooftop, "I'm the oldest person in the whole place." His voice was troubled.

*

Monkey Zheng had trained his monkey well, and all the children in Huajie enjoyed their antics. We often ran after him as he made his rounds, following him wherever he performed. He could get his monkey to count, to separate red and green beans, and even to circle around a woman three times and guess if she was married or not. The monkey wore different out-fits depending on the season, all of them alluring and brightly colored, making the monkey seem rather lewd. Along with the regular stuff—cycling, tumbling, bowing, holding hands—he had apparently also taught his monkey to masturbate in public, which made the men applaud and the women spit at him in disgust. That's the life of a monkey handler. I recalled how, after every performance, Monkey Zheng would toss his monkey over his shoulder, where it would dangle on his back. The only difference was the leash he had tied around its neck: a colorful cloth braid. That was an important part of the performance too. The monkey would twist like a carp then flip onto its master's shoulder to salute and bow to the audience as if it were the Great Sage. Only then, amid applause, would the monkey show truly be over.

Being older than the rest of us, Feng Nian had seen more monkey shows. Yet he couldn't remember thinking much about Monkey Zheng's performances before the nightmares began—at least not in the six years he'd been in Beijing.

"Have you seen any monkeys recently?" Xingjian asked.

"I went to the zoo a couple of years ago. There were monkeys there."

"There you go!" Xingjian took a book out from the cardboard box beneath his bed: *The Interpretation of Dreams* by some Westerner named Freud, its pages falling apart from how often he'd read it. Brandishing the book, he spoke in the stertorous voice of a professor. "Nian, you're repressed. Sex is weighing on you—or seeing those monkeys has awakened certain unspeakable memories."

"Would you stop talking about sex every time you open your mouth? Anyway, the monkeys were two years ago!"

"This Floyd guy says even memories of breastfeeding can have a lasting effect, never mind something that happened as recently as two years ago. Nian, bro, you're repressed. And sex is really important."

Of course, Xingjian wasn't going to stop talking about sex as long as he was brandishing that book. I don't know where he got hold of it, but he read it like porn. If there hadn't been a spicy sentence every few lines, who'd have the patience to read some foreigner's long-winded thoughts about dreams?

We didn't get to the bottom of it all, and Feng Nian kept having nightmares. He tried all kinds of tricks, such as staying up until he was nearly falling asleep on his feet, but even that didn't help. As soon as he drifted off, without any kind of transition he was a monkey in a suit, just like that. Oh, and have I mentioned the shoes? The six-eared macaque's shoes were buffed to a shine with Golden Rooster brand polish—a fly would slip off if it tried to land… He tried drinking himself into a stupor and got so smashed he thought he was Baolai, but when he lay down, his dreams were still of a six-eared macaque named Feng Nian. The following morning, as we jogged along, he said the chain around his neck had been so tight, he couldn't even throw up what he'd drunk and had to swallow it back down, which made his belly swell and woke him up. He also tried to squeeze out the macaque with other dreams—the night was only so long, and if he could dream of something else, there wouldn't be time for the nightmares. During the day, he would keep thinking about a bunch of strange things, hoping to shift the narrative—after all, as the Duke of Zhou once said, "As you think in the day, so you shall dream at night." Keeping his mind focused on one single thing all day, though, required so much time and concentration, it ended up being more exhausting than his job. Plus, it only worked occasionally—it was hardly worth the effort. He was suffering so much, he might as well have been dead. So he gave up.

*

Auntie Feng was pestering me again on the phone. She couldn't reach Feng Nian, so she had camped out at my parents' home waiting for me to call. The last time she'd spoken to him, he'd vaguely said something about "testing the waters." Then he'd hung up, and that was the last anyone heard from him. Now Auntie Feng was saying, "What crap, he grew up on this street, he knows how many hairs are on every person's head. What waters are there to test? You tell that son of a bitch to call me back—now, right away, immediately, no excuses!" So there I was, with another mission. I hustled my ass back to Hailong Electronics and yelled through the doorway, "Feng Nian! Now, right away…" etc. etc.

My shout ruined everything. Feng Nian was in the middle of showing a Canon camera to a customer, making it sound like the best thing since sliced bread. The guy was on the verge of pulling the trigger when I showed up. By the time I was finished passing along Auntie Feng's message, the customer had moved on to another sales clerk, and Feng Nian could only watch as he bought two single-lens reflex cameras from that other guy. After work, he came straight over to our pingfang and screamed at me like a maniac. "I told you not to come to the shop, and you still had to show up! I could have sold two single-lens reflexes!"

I ignored him. What was the big deal? It was just a couple of crappy cameras. I had plenty to grumble about too, but you didn't see me going off. He might not think it mattered where I jogged, but Zhongguancun has terrible traffic, and the air is awful—why had I been filling my lungs with pollution? Then there was Auntie Feng, stubborn as a terrier, sitting around in my parents' home all day waiting for the phone to ring, stressing out my mother. And Auntie Feng had to be kept company, which meant Ma couldn't do any chores except embroidering insoles. There were only three of us in the family—we didn't need that many insoles. Even Baolai got annoyed at Feng Nian. When Baolai says something is bad, there's definitely a problem—and if anyone has an issue with Baolai, well, that person is almost certainly bad news. Now Baolai was saying, "Nian, we're doing this for your own good."

Feng Nian rolled his eyes and sighed like a leaky balloon. "Forget it. You people wouldn't understand."

It's true, we didn't understand why he thought being set up was such torture. Later, he played Ace of Spades with us on the rooftop. The loser had to take a drink, and he got tipsy enough to stammer out the truth. The fact was, he really liked Zheng Xiaohe. He had been three grades above her in school, and when he'd had nothing to do, he would stroll past her classroom "by accident" to catch a glimpse of her, which always threw him into a tizzy. Even now, the thought of it made his face hot. Otherwise, he would have called long ago to turn her down. The other thing was, his shop was about to open a branch in Chaoyang district, and they were looking for an experienced, steady employee with a good sales record, particularly within the last two months, to be the manager there. Feng Nian had no problem with the first two requirements, and if he just managed to bring in a good haul, he'd be golden. Things hadn't been going great, though. Two fancy cameras and all their accessories sold for almost 50,000 yuan, and that would have put him over the top—you don't normally land a sale like that more than once a month.

"Oh," I said. I felt bad.

"This is my last chance." Feng Nian said, clutching his beer bottle like it was a karaoke mic. "I'll be thirty-one next month. When I arrived in Beijing, I told myself if I hadn't gotten anywhere by thirty, I'd head home, get fucking married, and have a kid. Come on, guys, bottoms up!"

He slept in late rather than going jogging the next morning. After washing up, he rushed to work. He'd had the same dream: him on the monkey-handler's back with the silver chain cutting so deep into his flesh he thought it would slice through his jugular and windpipe.

After that, he came running with me only occasionally, and his form wasn't great. I could understand that all this was hard for him. Anyone would have trouble finding the energy to jog after sleeping so badly. I even ended up having the same dream: I was a six-eared macaque, dressed in a jacket, jeans, and sneakers, hanging off someone's back. I thought I was going to suffocate; my face must have been swollen and flushed as a pumpkin. When I woke up, I cried for Feng Nian, my friend. But I had that dream only once. For him it was at least three times a week, each time more intense than before.

*

We decided to make an effort for Feng Nian. The four of us pooled our savings, which came to 3,000 yuan. Baolai said, "Well, that's better than nothing." We got one of Xingjian's friends to go to Hailong and find Feng Nian. His task was to buy anything he wanted, as long as he spent the whole 3,000. The guy went in and asked for Feng Nian, but a co-worker said Feng Nian was ill and he hadn't been in for a couple of days. The guy came charging back into our apartment, spitting fire—were we trying to punk him? Sending him in all guns blazing, but the target was gone!

Xingjian said, "Why didn't you tell us he was off sick?"

"How was I supposed to know?" I responded. "He doesn't go jogging every day."

Miluo's eyes widened. "Could it be that he…"

"That he what?"

Miluo waved it away. "Nothing. I'm talking crap."

Baolai and I exchanged glances. We stood up and went outside.

Two streets over, we pushed open the courtyard gate and found Feng Nian's door wide open. It was evening; the sky was darkening from the top down. It

was murky inside—the light was off. I started coughing from the smoke. Feng Nian sat on a broken rattan
chair, puffing away, his cigarette flickering like a little
ghost flame. I turned on the light. His hair was sticking out at odd angles, his eyes were sunken, his beard
wild. Right away, you knew he was a seasoned insom-
niac. He wore only long underwear; his suit and tie lay
rumpled on the bed, which was covered in stuff, as if
he'd just moved in.

"I was just coming to see you," said Feng Nian. The
hand with the cigarette gestured vaguely around the
room. "I'm taking the train home tonight. Have a look
around—if you see anything you like, help yourself."

"Nian, what's going on?" I tried to sound as relaxed
as I could.

"Nothing, I'm just going back to check it out," he
said. "I've managed to stay awake for two nights now,
so I haven't had any dreams. Lying awake in the dark,
I worked it all out: I should settle down with a good
woman and have a child with her." He began to cough
and went on till tears were streaming from his eyes.
Grabbing his dress shirt from the bed, he dabbed his
eyes with it. Next, he handed me a letter and asked
me to go over to Hailong when I had time and give it
to his manager or even just to one of his coworkers to
pass on.

Baolai and I sat on a bench across from him, helping ourselves to Zhongnanhai cigarettes from his pack.
Smoking's bad for the health and we kept coughing.
Baolai thought the light might be hurting Feng Nian's
eyes, so he turned it off. We sat there in silence.

Before we left, Feng Nian pointed at the closet

and said hesitantly, "Either of you want a suit?"

We shook our heads.

The next day, I went to Hailong. The deputy manager was there. He tore open the envelope and had just finished reading the letter when another besuited middle-aged man walked over. The deputy said, "Manager Li, no need for that chat with Feng Nian. He's handed in his notice."

"Just now?" Manager Li smacked his head and laughed. "That little bastard Feng sure knows how to pick his moment. We'll find someone else, then. Don't blame the government if your life's a mess."

As I was leaving, I bumped into the salesgirl from Tieling. She said, "Hey, aren't you Feng's friend? What are you doing here? Where's Feng? Oh, and that roast yam was delicious, thanks for that."

I smiled at her. "Have you ever had a suit-wearing nightmare?"

"What are you talking about?"

I realized it was a weird question, and ungrammatical too. She was clearly someone who slept soundly at night.

So I just said, "Nothing."

COMING
OF AGE

Coming of Age

"Okay, but you all keep quiet."

"Even while we're eating the cake?" I asked.

"You're the worst, blabbermouth," said Xingjian. "None of you interrupt me while I'm talking."

We nodded. We were having cake up on the rooftop, twenty candles stuck in the cream frosting.

"The first time I saw her was at the donkey-burger joint. I'd gone there for my usual order: four burgers, spicy pickles, a bowl of millet porridge. I was sitting, staring at an ant crawling diagonally across the table. Then a woman's voice: 'What would you like to eat?' I looked up. My first impression of her was clean-cut, fresh-faced, would look good in a white dress. But I was still annoyed: I'd been eating there for more than a year, and after the first three times, no one had ever had to ask what I wanted. But even though I've got a bad temper—Miluo knows it—I never blow up at strangers, particularly women."

"It's true," said Miluo. "I can confirm."

"I told you to keep quiet..." said Xingjian. "I told her the three things I wanted. She smiled and went back into the kitchen. She had a nice ass, round and full. Don't laugh. Two minutes later she brought out my dinner on a tray. Then she sat down by the front counter with her knees together and looked out the window like she had something on her mind. I was the only customer in the place; no one else eats dinner that early. After I ate, I was going to paste up ads—Chen Xingduo's daily quota was 5,000."

"That's total bullshit," said Miluo. "How the hell could you paste up 5,000 ads a day?"

"I didn't know any better; I was just starting out. He was working me into the ground. Now you've thrown me off—where was I?"

"Your early dinner," said Baolai.

"Right. It was just me in there the whole time. She was looking outside, and the afternoon sunlight lit up her profile, so the fine hairs all glowed. She was very pale, and her hair was pulled back in a ponytail. I'm trying to remember… Her hair was really black, no bangs. She looked like an oil painting, sitting there. Though I only dared to glance at her occasionally, I knew she wasn't looking at anything outside. Her eyes were unfocused and she had this little smile, like she was dreaming with her eyes open."

"When she smiled, she had dimples. And there was a mole on the left side of her neck," offered Miluo.

Xingjian glared at him, then picked up his bottle and took a big swig. Miluo shut up.

We were sitting on the roof as the sun went down. There were donkey burgers, spicy pickles, and millet porridge on the table, along with duck's neck, mala goose, pork cheeks, and beer. The cake was on a chair.

"Just thinking of that afternoon makes my guts

shiver, like I'm starving. She really was like an oil painting. Once I finally hit the big time, I'm going to find the best art teacher there is, and I'm going to paint that afternoon."

"Then what?"

"I finished my food and left."

That was it? All that rhapsodizing—and he just finished his food and left?

"So, I went back again the next afternoon. Honestly, until I walked through those doors again, I hadn't thought of her once since dinner the day before. She came over to serve me again, and I gave my usual order. Two minutes later she was out with the tray. She sat in the same seat as the day before, picked up a pen, and started drawing on a piece of paper on the counter. The sunlight hit her face, neck, and part of her shoulder. Her eyes were downcast, looking like another oil painting."

"Can't you find a new metaphor?" said Miluo. "I'm thinking she was sexy, like Gong Li."

"That isn't a metaphor," I corrected him.

"Well…was she like Gong Li, anyway?"

"Bullshit! Gong Li's flashy. This girl wouldn't deign to wear makeup," Xingjian said. "She looked like an oil painting to me, so what? If it bothers you, just eat your meat and drink your beer."

"We're not bothered," Baolai said. "I agree with Xingjian, she doesn't sound like the makeup type. Go on."

"When I was done eating, I left."

"Fuck! During dinner she's an oil painting, then you finish eating and you're out? Would it kill you to give us something to sink our teeth into?" Miluo was getting upset.

"Kids should be quiet while their elders are speaking. I haven't even gotten to the third time, have I?" said Xingjian. "It was this third time that I talked to her. I said, 'Where's Miss Ye? I haven't seen her around.' She said, 'Ye went home for a few days; I'm covering.' I responded, 'Oh, I owe her three kuai from before, should I just give it to you?' She said, 'Sure, I'll take it for her.'" Xingjian paused to take a bite of goose and pork cheek and to drink some beer.

The late August weather was just right, and birds were flying overhead. Not far from us, the skyscrapers of Beijing were spreading, quick as a tropical jungle. We were eating our meat and drinking our beer on the low roof of our single-story building, imagining love—which, Xingjian aside, hardly seemed to be in the cards for the other three of us. And even Xingjian's "her" seemed suspect. Shouldn't love be hotter and heavier?

"I didn't know if I liked her. I don't really know how to tell if I like someone. One time I was standing here on the roof, looking south, and I saw that Miss Ye's courtyard was totally empty. She lived in one of the rooms; the landlord had the other two. The landlord did some business over by Baishiqiao and came back a couple times a week at most, so Ye pretty much had the place to herself. I came down from the roof and went tottering off southward. As I passed Miss Ye's courtyard I pushed at the gate, but it was locked, so I stood against it and looked through a crack. Then I heard footsteps, but the gate opened before I could back away. It was her—she was startled too. I blushed red right down to my heels and started stuttering. 'Uh… I-I was just p-passing by and th-thought I'd see if Miss Ye was b-back.' She said, 'She's not back yet, I'm staying here now.' It didn't even occur to me to apologize, I just spun around and took off, wishing I could have simply vanished.

"It was days before I dared to go back to the donkey-burger place. She didn't ask what I wanted, just brought me my four burgers, spicy pickles, and millet porridge. When I was paying she asked, 'Where've you been?' I put my head down and said, 'Nowhere.' She handed over my change and said, 'Take care on the road.' She thought I'd been traveling. I was nearly crying on my way out—since coming to Beijing, no one but my own parents has ever said anything like that to me. I turned back and saw her looking through the window, smiling at me. She's older than me; that smile just hit me. Her mouth was small, but she had a nice broad smile; you could fit all the good things in the world into that smile. My guts suddenly twisted. She had me hooked."

"Have a smoke, then tell us more." Miluo lit it for him. "How'd you *get* it, exactly?"

Miluo made that "get" sound really suggestive; he wanted to get to the good part.

"Shut up, Miluo! You can talk shit about other girls, but watch it with her. I talk shit, too," Xingjian said. "I can be a bastard, but I'd never talk shit about her. You know what it means to 'profane' something, right? You read books. I need to keep something pure. I started going to the donkey-burger joint twice a day, until I was practically sick from it. After three days she said, 'They may be good but you can't pig out on them; you need some variety in your diet.' I nodded in response, 'Sure, you're right.' When she wasn't at work, I'd climb up on the roof so I could see her coming home, walking around the courtyard, doing laundry, going in and out of her room. Occasionally I'd see her dumping the wash water out, not wearing much."

"I remember now," said Baolai. "For a while there you'd come back from pasting ads, and no matter how late it was, you'd go up on the roof and wander around—is that what you were doing? I'd wonder, is he up there in the middle of the night composing poetry or what?"

"Yeah, I remember too," said Miluo. "Tell us the truth now, Xingjian: How little was she wearing?"

"Sometimes just her underwear, other times not even that. Pale all over. What? Get hard? Of course it got hard, I'm a goddamn man not a block of wood. Seeing her body made me want it. My empty days finally had something to them. That's when I realized that I was eighteen and I'd started desiring women."

"So, when was it that you, you know…" I slowly tapped my forefingers together; they got it.

"Where'd you learn about that, little guy?" Miluo laughed at me.

I clinked my beer bottle against his and took a gulp. We'd grown up fast, working away from home, and had had to face the world and all its temptations on our own. We had no one to rely on, no one to share our burdens; we knew we had to take care of ourselves.

I'd been in Beijing only a few months, but it had felt like a crash course in how to face all that life required.

"It wasn't until my birthday."

"So, a year ago today. What about before that?"

"Life as usual."

"Boooriiiing. The goods! Give us the goods!"

"It's hardly enough to call it 'goods,'" Xingjian said. "You've all been alive seventeen, eighteen years— how much 'goods' have you gotten? Back then it wasn't like now, when we all know what the goal is and we're just in a rush to get there. Back then I was in the middle of a frustrating but beautiful quest, like I was being drawn on by some distant scent. Something delicate and faint. Once I caught that scent I couldn't let it go, but I couldn't just snatch hold of it, either. Everything went on as usual: I'd to the donkey-burger place and see her; my brain and body were filled with her; I'd pass by her home again and again, melancholy and even tragic. Every time I saw her or walked by her gate my heart would pound in my chest... What do you say, maybe I should read a few more books and become a fucking poet?"

"You should write fiction," I said. "You're as long-winded as a novelist."

Miluo and Baolai grinned. Xingjian laughed too.

"What can I say? Do you really want to hear that I was going to write her love letters? I wrote them, and then I tore them up. I wrote down all the things I didn't dare say to her face—'I want you,' 'I love you,'—I even cried. Still I tore them up. Didn't dare show anyone. In love everyone is a poet, but everyone's also a thief. What's more, it was secret and unrequited. She barely knew I existed; she never thought of me. I couldn't blame her: I was just a regular who liked donkey burgers, a stupid kid. But I was almost nineteen! I was timid as a mouse—and then came my birthday."

"Me and Baolai threw you a party," said Miluo. "You insisted on blowing out your birthday candles at the donkey-burger joint."

"You're the first person in the world to celebrate your birthday with donkey burgers," Baolai said.

"We brought the cake over to the burger joint, but it turned out she wasn't working that day," Xingjian said. "I was pretty disappointed at first, but then my sorrow seemed to give me a kind of strength, and I ate a whole lot of meat and drank a whole lot of booze. You two have never seen me drink so much, right? You thought I was drunk? You think that little bit could put me down? Sure, after the cake I put my head down on the table for a while, but I was just trying to get you two to leave so I could be alone with my sorrow. I was nineteen. I used to think nineteen was a long way off, but there it was, right in front of me, in that Beijing burger joint a million miles from home and family, thinking about a girl I didn't even know. I put my head down and cried until my sleeve was wet. Then I stood up, picked up the rest of the cake… Hang on, I need a drink." Xingjian opened another bottle of Yanjing beer and drained half of it in one go.

"Then what?"

"I went to her courtyard and started knocking on the gate."

*

"Who's there?" she asked.

"I brought you something to eat," said Xingjian. He kept his eyes wide; that was the only way to maintain his courage. The seven bottles of beer he'd drunk were weighing down his eyelids, but if he let them drift shut he worried he might start crying.

She led him inside. The alcohol had left him with a stuffed-up nose, but Xingjian could still smell a wonderful scent, something unlike regular face powder. Her long hair was spread across her shoulders; she was wearing slippers, her pale bare heels turned out slightly. The fluorescent lights elongated her shadow; he was in fact a half head taller than her. There was only one chair, and Xingjian sat in it, still holding the cake. She sat on the bed, legs together, slippers dangling casually from her toes. The sheets were sky blue. An open book was face down on the bedside table. She looked at him the same way she had looked out the shop window, with a half-smile. Xingjian avoided her gaze, struggling to keep his eyes open. He stood and brought the cake to her, saying:

"I'm nineteen now."

She took the cake from him, scooped a bit of frosting from the top and dipped her finger in her mouth. "Fluffy and sweet," she said. "So, you're nineteen." She put another bit of frosting in her mouth, looking at his hands where they hung at his sides, trembling. She stared for a full two minutes. That was how it felt to

Xingjian, anyway—the minutes were stretching into hours, and he didn't know if he should stay there or sit back down. "I'll give you a present," she said. "Shut the door."

He did as she asked. She motioned him over, and Xingjian came back to the bedside. She wiped her fingers with a tissue and started to undo his shirt.

It still seems like a dream to Xingjian. He'd poured seven bottles of beer into his head, leaving it heavy and wobbling. He'd rehearsed that moment countless times in dreams and his imagination, oftentimes with her starring in his fantasies, when he could analyze the various steps like a pro. Now, faced with reality, the only certainty was that he was drunk. The alcohol had filled his head with paste; his whole body was trembling. All he could remember later was that she'd laid down, naked, and said to him:

"Get on top of me. Breathe deeply. Do what I say."

It was like drowning—difficult, drawn out yet somehow brief, a kind of suffocating beauty. When he ejaculated he seemed entirely suffused with electricity, glowing fire red, an explosion that started in his scalp and swept through his entire body. He lay atop her, tears running from his eyes. It was the first time since coming to Beijing that he'd felt such overwhelming homesickness.

She stroked his back and said, "Good, that's right."

He knew he'd screwed it up; it was over before she'd even made a sound. But as she cleaned up she still said, "That was great."

Dressed again, she sat on the bed and he returned

to the chair, as if they'd never moved at all.

"You always stand on the roof and watch me," she said.

Xingjian said nothing.

"I asked Ye; she doesn't remember you owing her three kuai."

"I really did."

"Okay," she laughed. "How long have you been in Beijing?"

"A year."

"You're so young. Why aren't you in school?"

"Couldn't hack it. I left home with a relative."

"You're still young."

"I'm nineteen."

"I know…" she laughed. "I mean, you don't know why you left home?"

Xingjian hadn't thought about it in those terms. When he'd dropped out of school his family said he couldn't just hang around the house, he had to go out and start working, it would break him in. So, he'd come to Beijing, where his uncle Chen Xingduo happened to be. If he'd been in Shanghai, or Guangzhou, or Nanjing instead, well then at this moment Xingjian would simply be living in some little room in Shanghai, Guangzhou, or Nanjing.

"When I was eighteen, I graduated from teacher's college and started teaching Chinese at an elementary school in the local township," she said. "The farthest I'd gone then was to school in the city, forty-five kilometers from home. I wanted to go someplace farther. The county town had a small station with a train to Beijing every other day. I'd wanted to take that train since I was a kid, to go as far away as I could, but I didn't know *why* I wanted to go so far away. All the way till graduation I still hadn't ever taken a train... I've got a story; do you want to hear it?"

"Uh-huh."

"The elementary school was a red-roofed building with broken windows, and my classroom held forty students. There was a middle school next door that had just been sent a college student from Beijing— they said from Peking University—who'd committed errors: blocking traffic, giving speeches, handing out pamphlets. We heard it was pure luck that he hadn't been thrown in jail. But he was a good teacher, always reading; he knew all kinds of characters we'd never seen before. My supervisor knew him well and often asked me to borrow books from him or ask him things, so I got to know him, too. Handsome? Ha, not as handsome as you. But he was a good guy. He didn't smile much, going around with a wooden face. We all knew he was bitter, but who wouldn't be, in his place? The township was too small for a smart guy like him, but there wasn't anywhere else for him to go, and it looked like he might spend the rest of his life with us. He told me I should get out and see the world. I asked where I should go, and he said anywhere. Just don't squat in that pigsty. That's something we say back home: holing up in one place like a pig in its pen, going nowhere, daring nothing, until they drag you to the slaughterhouse.

"Maybe you've guessed that, yes, I liked him. I'm not ashamed. Of course I was awfully shy about it; I was just a young girl. The day I turned nineteen I went to see him—it was Dragon Boat Festival and his roommate had gone back home to celebrate; he was there all alone, reading. We were together that night. I cried a bit, but I was also very happy—it was what I wanted. As a birthday present, he gave me two books and the same piece of advice he'd given me many times before: Get out and see the world... Are you sleepy?"

"No," Xingjian said, concentrating all his strength on keeping his eyes open. His eyelids were heavy, but he was clear-headed. "Go on, I'm listening."

"A year later he left to attend a graduate program. I knew he would leave eventually. A person like that could do anything he wanted, given the opportunity. I kept teaching in town. I read the books he gave me. I'm not much of a student, and I didn't understand a lot of what I read. But I gradually realized what he meant by getting out and seeing things. I wanted more and more to get out. Nothing too ambitious, I just wanted to go someplace far away. He and I didn't stay in contact, and a year later I got a boyfriend, someone I worked with. We got along really well and our parents were pleased with the match, so we started talking long term. One day I went to the county seat to buy school supplies and passed the station just as the Beijing train happened to be pulling out, like a charging bull with white smoke coming from its head. All of a sudden I felt terrible, and tears started flowing. When I got back to the school, I told my boyfriend I wanted to go to Beijing."

"What did he say?"

"He said, 'Okay, let's go together during summer break. We can see the Forbidden City, Tiananmen, and the Great Wall.' But I didn't mean to go sight-seeing, right? I wanted to stay there, I wanted to go right away, I couldn't wait another day. He didn't understand; we started fighting. He was blowing up, but I stayed quiet. In the end, he tied a backpack and a suitcase to his motorcycle and took me to the station. I sat by the window, holding my pack; he stood on the platform with the suitcase at his feet. He wouldn't pass it through the window—he hoped I would come to get it, and then not get back on. Finally, he left the suitcase on the platform, looked at his watch, and said, 'I'll wait for you outside the station; if you don't come in five minutes I'm going home.' The train was leaving in three minutes. He disappeared from the platform. I got off the train, grabbed the handle of the suitcase, and just stood there. The train slowly started moving, and I walked alongside it. A conductor was about to close the door, and yelled, 'Are you getting on or not?' I started to run."

"Did you get on?"

"No. When I came out of the station more than ten minutes later, my boyfriend was gone."

"So you went home."

"I stayed in the county town a couple of nights and then took another train to Beijing."

"And you've been here ever since."

"Ever since."

"Did…did you look for the college student?"

"No. I've just lived; I just did what I could. Found work in the corners of Beijing, lived my life. The restaurant will be my last job here."

"You're planning to…"

"Go home, yes. It's been more than six years; it's time."

"Do you have to go?"

She nodded.

"What's wrong with Beijing?"

"You don't get it. At a certain point, you need to start listening to yourself, listening to your truest desires, no matter what they are. I want to go home."

"Did Miss Ye go home, too?"

"Your 'Miss Ye'...yeah. When Ye decided to leave I thought to myself: She's been beaten, she's giving up, she lost. She couldn't take it, but I can. Later, though, I understood. Staying or going isn't a test of will; it's beyond your control. And going home is actually the more difficult choice." She picked up the face-down book, whose cover had been wrapped in blank paper. "This book says that France once had the best homing pigeons. They'd release them from the front lines in wartime to carry news back home. They'd have to fly over the entire battlefield, not looking down the whole way or they'd never reach home. Can you imagine? Flying over horrible, blood-soaked battlefields, only looking forward. Do you understand?"

Xingjian didn't, and in that instant he found the courage to admit it. "I don't get it," he said.

"I'm talking about Ye's courage. It's hard to leave home, but it's even harder to go back. Is there anything braver than crossing a battlefield with your head up, eyes straight ahead?"

"I understand," Xingjian said.

"You're only able to imagine it. Someday, you'll *get* it."

*

"I'm still a little confused," said Miluo.

"Someday, you'll get it," said Xingjian.

"Quit blowing smoke," snorted Miluo. "I can't be bothered."

"What happened then?" I asked.

"I left, and she went to bed."

"I mean, is there more to the story?"

"Nothing else. I kept getting dinner at the donkey-burger joint for the next couple of days, and she would still sit at the counter, looking out the window. Nothing unnecessary was said. Everything that shouldn't be said is unnecessary. In the evening, I'd pass her gate, but every time I pushed at it, it was bolted. A few more days passed, and I decided to stop overthinking it—all I wanted was to hear her talk. She'd said, 'You should listen to your deepest desires.' So I knocked on the gate. It was ages before it opened, and there was the landlord standing in front of me, yawning. I asked, 'Where is she?' The landlord answered, 'She who?' 'Your tenant.' 'Oh, her. She gave up the room and went home.'"

I knew the story was pretty much over, but couldn't help asking, "What then?"

"Then nothing. I never saw her again."

Miluo started counting on his fingers. "You all keep quiet; I'm figuring this out. No wonder Xingjian likes older women. She was twenty-eight, wasn't she?"

"I didn't ask," said Xingjian.

"Well, what was her name?" asked Baolai.

"I don't know."

"Shit, you slept with her and never knew a thing."

"Shut the hell up, Miluo! Keep up that bullshit and you better believe we're going to have a problem!"

For a moment all was quiet on the roof, with only the sound of the evening wind passing through the persimmon tree in the courtyard.

"Okay then," Baolai said. "Xingjian's twenty now; time for candles and cake."

Then we were cheerful again, gathered around the cake and blocking the wind from all sides as we lit twenty candles. The little flames flickered and danced.

Miluo said, "I'm not bullshitting this time, Xingjian—what do you want to do now that you're twenty?"

"I want to get serious," said Xingjian. "To put down roots in Beijing."

Then it was time to blow out the candles. Xingjian closed his eyes, but once they were closed he realized that he didn't really know what wish to make. In his mind he moved southwest, toward that other court-yard, and then he opened his eyes and blew out the candles. The sky went dark.

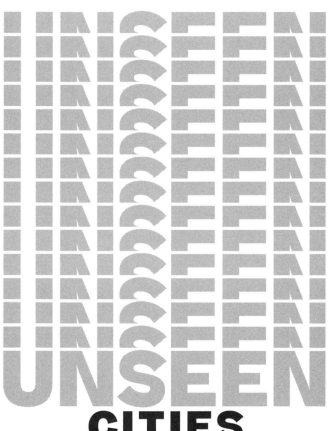

Unseen Cities

1

Tianxiu died on the night of the Mid-Autumn Festival. When we got there he was lying on the ground, body all twisted up, fingers splayed wide, blood trickling into his staring eyes, staining the full moon red. The Guizhou crew was long gone, and only Tianxiu's co-workers were still around. One of them squatted on the curb with his head in his hands, while the other two stood with us, in front of the corpse, pounding their fists into their palms and cursing the viciousness of the Guizhou men: *You dogfuckers better watch out—unless you grow wings and fly away, you're dead meat, we'll fuck you up one by one or two by two.* No one touched Tianxiu because one of the co-workers, a streetwise guy, said we had to preserve the scene of the crime so the police could gather evidence. We all knew he was dead—his forehead had been caved in, and once he fell to the ground, the Guizhou guy stomped on his stomach with his heavy leather boots. Tianxiu had curled up like a giant shrimp, arms wrapped around his belly, head touching his knees. Then, like a taut

51

string snapping, his head lolled to one side and his face turned to the sky, and with that reddening moon as his last sight, he grew completely still. Big Six, who'd come to find us a few minutes ago, said he'd put his hand on Tianxiu's forehead and it had been as soft as a roast yam.

When Big Six ran into the courtyard, we were all on the rooftop eating mooncakes. Thirty Thou Hong and Chen Xingduo had, in a fit of generosity, given us Mid-Autumn off. For once we wouldn't be spending the night pasting ads around the neighborhood. We were each given thirty yuan too, to celebrate the holiday. We pooled the cash and bought mooncakes, duck necks, pig cheeks, donkey burgers, and beer, all of which we devoured while gazing at the sky. The moon was always brilliant on the fifteenth of the eighth month, illuminating the courtyard as bright as if it were day. Big Six came dashing down the alleyway, panting hard, and burst through our gate shouting, "Tianxiu's dead, and you're still stuffing yourselves!"

My legs went weak at those words, and I was no longer able to even lift the beer bottle to my mouth. "Dead," Big Six repeated, "it's true!" Then he spread his hand and smacked his forehead. It took Baolai, Xingjian, and Miluo some effort to get me down off the roof. My legs didn't feel sturdy again until I was back on the ground. We ran eastward, toward the center of Beijing, against the direction of its sprawl.

The police had already been called, and an officer in a peaked cap was standing at the street. The co-worker of Tinaxiu's who'd gone to inform their boss wasn't back yet. Someone else said the boss and a few of the foremen had gone for a celebratory dinner—nobody was sure where, but people were going around to all the restaurants.

"It was all because of that crappy telephone!" said Big Six, gesturing at the public phone at the curb, its stainless steel receiver dangling forlornly just above the ground. "Tianxiu was waiting for his wife to call back, but that Guizhou bastard couldn't wait even a minute—he just butted in there and snatched it from him."

Tianxiu had already called a few minutes prior, and his wife had been telling him their son had learned how to say "Baba" a few days ago and was excitedly calling everyone he saw "Baba." That got Tianxiu all choked up. His kid was a year and a half old, and he'd already called his mother Mama and his grandparents Yeye and Nainai, but the word *Baba* hadn't passed his lips yet. Everybody said the most intelligent kids come to language late, but that's the sort of crap you console other people with; no one believes it about their own child. Tianxiu wanted to hear the boy say it for himself, so his wife told him she'd call him back in a couple of minutes—she just had to run and get the boy from her in-laws'. A minute passed, and Tianxiu could practically see his wife scurrying back to the phone, their son in her arms. Then the Guizhou guy waiting in line behind him lost his patience, reached past Tianxiu's shoulder, and grabbed the receiver.

"Just one more minute," Tianxiu protested.

"Another minute? You're killing me."

Tianxiu held up his index finger. "One minute. My son's learned to say Baba!"

"What the fuck's that to me?" the Guizhou guy said, shoving him aside. "He's not calling *me* Baba, is he?"

Big Six said it was entirely possible Tianxiu hadn't really meant to snatch the receiver back, but he'd been knocked off balance by the Guizhou guy and would have landed on his ass if he hadn't grabbed hold of something. Which happened to be the phone. The Guizhou guy took it as a challenge and the two of them got into it, but passers-by quickly separated them. There were maybe three to five men on each side; all of them had been enjoying the holiday, wandering the streets after their booze and mooncakes, gazing up at the full moon. They were all construction workers, from the building site a block away from Tianxiu and Big Six's. You'd hear accents like theirs from time to time; it made them seem familiar even though they were strangers. After the two men were pulled apart, everybody should have gone their separate ways and that would have been that, but the Guizhou guy insisted on grumbling, "If you want to hear him call you Baba, why are you working here in Beijing? Shit, you aren't fit to be a father!"

"Not fit how? He's my son," said Tianxiu, perplexed.

"You just aren't."

"But how?"

"You just aren't!"

The two grown men traded a few more gibes, and their rage built. Virtually at the same moment, they wrestled free and launched themselves at each other like fighting roosters. While trying to mediate, their co-workers began squabbling too, and soon the scene descended into a brawl. The Guizhou guy snatched up a loose piece of concrete and drove it into Tianxiu's forehead. Tianxiu collapsed onto his back in slow motion like in a movie, his blood gleaming darkly in the moonlight. Everyone froze. Before anyone could react, the Guizhou guy's leather boots had stomped their victim and were making tracks, his five Guizhou compatriots dragging him away.

So that left Big Six and the others huddled around Tianxiu, calling his name. Blood was flowing into his eyes. And that's how Tianxiu, a man from my hometown, met his end at the age of thirty-seven.

2

I was closer to Tianxiu than to anyone else in the neighborhood. Back home in Huajie, our families' courtyards were next door, and when I was still in school, I'd bang on his window whenever I had a math problem I couldn't solve. Tianxiu was good at science—"extraordinarily good" according to my aunt, who'd been his classmate. Tianxiu had shown more promise than anyone else in their year, but he never got into university. He retook the entrance exam four years in a row and failed each time. Even his weakest classmates, some of whom had repeated all four years alongside him, made it into our local remote-learning school. After Tianxiu had given up completely and returned to Huajie in his thick glasses, we found out he'd set his sights way too high: he refused to study anywhere but in a big city, at one of China's finest universities. You could say he went down in a blaze of glory. No one blamed him. Those thick glasses alone made him a bit of a celebrity in Huajie; parents would point him out to their kids: *Just look at our Tianxiu!*

Anyone who needed glasses was clearly an intellectual, and thick lenses meant you were a total brainiac. Huajie had its share of reading glasses for the elderly, and pretentious sunglasses like toad eyes, but only Tianxiu was truly nearsighted. As a kid, I used to count the number of rings I could see reflected off his lenses, but the number would change whenever I shifted my angle. Tianxiu really was good at math, though. I'd slip all the questions I hadn't understood in class through his window, and he'd efficiently work through them, handing me the answers written out straightforwardly, far easier to understand than my teacher had ever managed, music blaring the whole time.

He bought a secondhand stereo, and for years he listened all day to his flashy cassette tapes. My parents didn't like those songs—all that shrieking, the *ooh ahs*, the wild-haired singers tossing their heads. The music didn't strike me as particularly good either, but I enjoyed the commotion, one person singing with the force of a few hundred screaming—that was art. And so, whenever I slipped out and snuck over to his place, once I'd finished asking him my math questions, I'd sit in the sun by his gate, listening to one singer sounding like many. Tianxiu's family had a huge yard, perfect for lounging against the wall on sunny winter mornings. That was Tianxiu in a nutshell, a guy who liked to bask in the winter sun. He'd shuffle around in his handmade black cloth shoes, their laces long missing, showing his nylon-sock-clad feet; his padded jacket would be haphazardly buttoned—or sometimes completely unbuttoned—one side wrapped over the other and his hands pulled up into the sleeves. All he needed was a piece of straw to complete his country bumpkin look. He seldom combed his hair, and it rose in greasy tufts from his head, poking out in every direction. He had a photo book of skyscrapers that he'd flip through, then he'd put it on the stone step outside his front door, place his glasses on the book, and cover his face with his hands, rubbing his eyes while looking up at the sun. He would do that for half an hour without making a sound, and I always thought he must be crying behind his hands, but he wasn't. The music would blast, *ooh ooh ah ah*, and when he lowered his hands it was as if he'd just woken up, refreshed from a deep sleep. "Ah," he'd say to me, "you're still here."

Tianxiu was nineteen years older than me, and to him I was definitely just a snot-nosed brat. Naturally he ignored me for the most part, but it wouldn't have made much difference even if he had paid me any attention—the ways in which adults lived their lives was incomprehensible to us kids. His life back then seemed carefree, but later I'd realize it must have been filled with tragic solitude. He slept late every day, and when he finally got up, he either sat in the sun with a book or shuffled his way down one of our main roads—Huajie Street, Great East Street, Great West Street, Great South Street—always alone, his shadow long and slender. With his scholar's face, he looked respectable even with that sagging gait. He'd stop along the way for a game of billiards, but he seldom talked, not even giving a practice stroke, just squinting and shooting out his cue, ricocheting the ball back and forth till it finally fell into a pocket. He'd studied enough geometry to work out the most scientifically proven angles across the table. He won quite a bit of money that way. With his billiards earnings in hand, he'd jump onto the old Golden Deer bicycle his father had bought in Shandong's Linyi City and take off in a random direction from Huajie, sometimes disappearing for two or three days at a time, reaching cities a hundred miles away before riding back.

Back in high school, I'd never been more than twenty miles from the village, and there was no way I could have guessed where he'd gone, or what he'd seen while he was there. It was always a city, anyway; I was sure of that. Tianxiu's mother often chatted with mine through our window, and she'd say he'd gone off to such-and-such a place, always wandering. She seemed unhappy about it, but Ma would try to console her with her blind worship of intellectuals: "Let him go, he has his own way of thinking."

"What way of thinking is that?" Tianxiu's ma retorted. "When he's done eating, he goes straight to sleep. I never see him smile, and I never see him cry. This has been going on for long enough, and it's not like he's the only one not going to college."

It was true. By then, several years after his last attempt at the college entrance exam, even his despair and resentment had faded away. He wasn't the only person in the world who'd failed five times: Fan Cang from Great West Street had been in the same boat, but Fan

Cang was back at home doing an honest day's work, growing carrots that earned him enough to live on.

Tianxiu's ma sighed. "Spoiled brat."

"But…"

This trailing off was indicative of the prevalent attitude in Huajie: If a bespectacled person was idle, he must have his reasons.

Late one night, my father came running in, breathing hard. As soon as he got through the front door, he rubbed his chest and said, "Thank god, I almost didn't make it." He'd been at the home of Twisty Meng from the rice shop watching a mahjong game when the police burst in to arrest the gamblers. Luckily my father was quick-witted enough to jump out the window. "Only Tianxiu and I escaped. Everyone else got arrested."

That was how I learned that Tianxiu was a gambler. "He's a master," said my father. "The way he counts tiles—his brain's as good as a computer." My father would go around the table looking at everyone's tiles, but he couldn't make sense of it all. Tianxiu only had to glance at his own hand to instantly calculate his odds. Tianxiu could gamble day and night without pausing to eat or drink, holding in his pee for up to ten hours. He won much more than he lost, and when he cashed out, hardly anyone complained—they all acknowledged that he'd had them beat. After all, he had four eyes, and they only had two. So, he'd go through an intense gambling session and leave with a pile of cash. A couple of days after that, his ma would be at the window, saying to mine, "He's gone again."

"Where to this time?"

"Who knows? He took his big backpack, said he'd be gone two weeks."

After I moved to Beijing, Tianxiu came to visit me and I asked what places he'd gone to over all those years. He laughed. "I just let my legs take me wherever they liked."

"What did you see?"

"I've forgotten. It's all in the past."

Tianxiu's life back then was the opposite of most Huajie men's, who enlisted on the boats to make money, which they'd spend when they got home. He only left home when he had enough cash and came back to make some more gambling when he'd spent it all.

The year he turned twenty-nine, Tianxiu surprised us all by quitting his long trips. All day long he'd wander the farm fields around Eight Roads, hands clasped behind his back. And there was one other major change: He stopped wearing glasses. Now he felt like a stranger to us. All those years of nearsightedness had caused his eyes to shrink back into their sockets, and he looked as if a different person had taken up residence in his body. He had to squint to recognize anyone. One autumn evening, his ma came to our window, dinner bowl still in her hand, and called to mine.

"Tianxiu's going to head up a production brigade," she said. "We're country folk, after all, and generations before him have done the same. He's set on it, and his father and I feel good about it. And his aunt has a girl lined up for our Tianxiu too!"

3

For a long time, I couldn't wrap my head around it: a failed scholar, a wastrel, a gambler, a wandering soul, eventually a newly glasses-less production brigade leader, was now a construction worker on the western edge of Beijing. How did he do it? After I'd arrived, Tianxiu and his coworker Big Six came to visit me and we sat together, chatting on the rooftop. In the distance, we could see Beijing's skyscrapers marching toward us. "The city is a giant bulldozer," said Big Six in his Shandong accent, echoing Tianxiu. "It's a plague—no one can win against it." I didn't care about any of that. Instead, I asked Tianxiu how he'd ended up working construction.

"If I can be a production brigade leader, why not a construction worker?"

"Speaking of which…why *did* you become a production brigade leader?"

"Too many people on the road," said Tianxiu. "Too crowded. I got tired of moving around."

"But now you've left again, right?"

"That's easy to explain," Big Six interrupted. "He's rested now. Isn't that right, Tianxiu? Ha!"

"Back then, there were really too many people heading for the cities. Where there was one, you'd find a bunch." Tianxiu twirled a Zhongnanhai between his fingers. "All searching for money. By the side of a river in Wuhan, I suddenly felt so very tired that I had to sit on the ground. A wave splashed all the way up to my neck, and I still couldn't be bothered to move. I'd gotten wet, so what. Darkness fell and a cold wind came along, but I just sat there shivering. Finally, I called a trishaw to take me back to the hotel. My driver was a man from Yichang who'd leased his family's land for other people to farm while he earned his living giving rides—it paid better, but he felt like he was drifting, and at night he would often dream that he was suspended in mid-air, pedaling away but not moving. While giving me a ride, he was so busy talking that he didn't notice a sharp turn in the road until there was a steep slope right in front of us. He slammed on the brakes, but we went head over heels. He split his lip and snapped a front tooth in half. I told him to go to the hospital, but he said he was fine. He fished a newspaper from his basket, crumpled it up, and pressed it to his mouth. 'Let's get you back to the hotel,' he said."

"And did he?" Big Six asked. They'd been working together for two years, but he'd never heard this story from Tianxiu.

"Obviously I couldn't let him. I gave him all the cash I had on me, still dripping from the river. By the time I'd walked back to my hotel, I'd come down with a cold. Took the train home with a high fever. Just like that, I no longer wanted to roam. Would it kill me to spend my whole life in Huajie after all? My grandpa was a farmer, and so was my father. Why couldn't I do the same? They happened to be looking for a production brigade leader, so I told them I'd read a few books about agriculture and I'd like to give it a try. I got the job, which turned out to be more about managing people. When work came up, you just had to holler at folks to get it done."

Plenty of people were leaving for the city back then, and the wave would probably keep swelling for years to come. And so, Tianxiu had also ended up in Beijing.

Two years ago, he'd come to Beijing as part of a Shandong construction crew. I was in high school at the time, living in the dorms. On a visit back home for the holidays, I was doing my homework and came upon a math problem I couldn't solve, so I tapped on Tianxiu's back window as usual. His wife opened the window and told me he was putting up buildings in Beijing. She said "Beijing" and "putting up buildings" with such reverence, you'd have thought he was working on a second Tiananmen Gate.

"So he's not a brigade leader anymore?"

"Who ever made real money from the soil?" said his wife. "Look around. Everyone's gone to the cities."

His wife hadn't actually wanted him to come to Beijing, particularly now that they had a kid. She was ten years younger than him and enjoyed having a daddy figure around to take care of her. Even so, Tianxiu decided he couldn't stay. Fine, then. His wife was tired of seeing him trudge around all day with a face like a coffin, and they really did need the cash, so ultimately she gritted her teeth and let him go. All the men around had gone off too, and at least hers was heading to Beijing—that was pretty impressive.

"It wasn't just about earning money." Tianxiu said, lighting his Zhongnanhai. "Gold doesn't grow from the ground, so farming was just making everyone poorer and poorer. I'd had enough. Or maybe that's not it exactly…working construction isn't bad, anyway. Mix cement to make concrete and reinforce it with steel, slap it on, and stack the bricks on top. Watch it get taller, bit by bit. The city? When I'm doing hard manual labor, I don't think about the city—I'm just making a building. Like when you solve a math problem, you're not taking an exam. Oh right, I forgot, you paste up ads for Thirty Thou Hong these days… Anyway, if I stop to think how I'm constructing this city, I feel as if I'm driving a giant excavator, wiping out everything that isn't a skyscraper. Like I'm erasing a whole page of writing. If you keep on thinking of the exam instead of just solving math problems, you'd get overwhelmed too."

To be honest, I was already overwhelmed—I didn't really understand what he was talking about. My job was sticking up small ads to promote my uncle Thirty Thou Hong's fake ID business—I no longer had any exams to take.

At the window in the village, Tianxiu's wife had said, "He needs to earn money. How else are we supposed to raise this kid?"

"Women never say what they really mean," said Tianxiu. "Who goes around thinking about money all day? Did you meet my son?"

"I played with him every day," I said. "Why did you name him Yulou? Jade Tower. Makes him sound like an opera singer or something."

"His father does build towers, after all," said Tianxiu.

4

Three days after the assault, Tianxiu's family arrived in Beijing.

I went with Big Six and the others to take his wife, son, and parents to see the spot where it happened. The phone looked exactly like it had before. A chunk was missing out of the sidewalk. Where Tianxiu had lain, you could still see the faint chalk outline the police had drawn around him, and dark streaks where his blood had seeped into the cement. His wife burst into loud sobs. Baolai and Big Six held up Tianxiu's parents while I carried Yulou. The poor kid had no idea what was going on. The city's suburbs alone must have seemed like a surreal diorama to him. He turned to me and solemnly said, "Baba!"

"Yulou," I said quietly, "Don't call me that, okay?"

The little boy stared as his weeping mother, turned back to me, puzzled, and called out again, "Baba!"

This reminded Yulou's mother and grandparents that the boy's baba would never be seen again. Now all three of them were howling, their bodies slowly sinking to the ground until they were kneeling by the chalk outline. As if it were actually their husband and son, their fingernails scrabbled at the cement, futilely trying to raise him off the ground. It's so easy for a person to die, but death can also be very abstract. This was their final sight of Tianxiu. They'd seen his corpse just before it was cremated, his body sliced apart and sewn back together, all his wounds concealed. His eyes were shut, the blood that had pooled in his sockets long since wiped away. He'd looked sound asleep, as if he'd never sustained a single injury. The autopsy had said his head injuries were sufficient to cause death, and so were the ones to his torso—his liver and gall bladder had been ruptured by the leather boots.

It hadn't taken much effort to arrest the Guizhou guy. The police went to the train station and found him smoking in the waiting room toilet. When he saw the officers, he said, "Hang on a minute, just at least let me finish." He drew on the cigarette manically, his last few drags so deep that he choked and coughed. He didn't quite believe Tianxiu was dead. When they confirmed this to be the case, he said to the officers, "So he died, just like that." Then he said, "Okay, so he's dead. I'll pay for it with my life." He didn't try to deny it at all.

When his co-workers had dragged him away, he'd been so annoyed—so what if he'd had a bit of a fight, hit someone with a chunk of cement? Then his co-workers told him to run, and the building site foreman said the same thing, but he wondered why he'd bother running; it's not like anyone died. Fights like these were very common on construction sites, big group brawls too; they were all used to it. Soon after that, a worker the foreman had sent to find out more came back and said, "Looks like he's dead: he's just lying there, not moving, and I heard they've called the police." That's when the guy had to take it seriously. The foreman ordered him to leave right away, that very instant: "Don't even stop to pack your stuff; don't cause problems for the company." Just before he left, the foreman reached into his wallet and handed over two months' wages. The guy got a cab to the train station—it was such a long way from the work site to the station, that was the most extravagant taxi ride of his life. His co-workers had told him he could go absolutely anywhere, except back home to Guizhou, and he'd agreed. When he bought his ticket, though, he changed his mind. Later, the police asked why he'd decided to return to Guizhou, and he said, "I had to see my parents and my son. If I really had killed someone, I'd spend the rest of my life on the run, and who knows when we'd ever see each other again?"

The officer said, "You didn't think you'd get caught?"

"Maybe I'd get caught. A life for a life. What else is there to do?"

I gleaned bits and pieces of news from Big Six, and it seemed he really was that calm. It's not like he wasn't scared of dying—he was shivering all over, and his hands shook as they cuffed him—but his mouth remained stubborn, reeking pure gunpowder every time he opened it, as if he had a grudge against everyone. He admitted his guilt but insisted he had no regrets. "I wasn't happy—in fact, I was furious, so I lashed out," he said. "He hit me too. It's just that, in the end, it was him who died, not me."

The officer said, "All because you couldn't wait one minute?"

"Isn't one minute enough of a reason?"

"And why did you say he wasn't fit to be a father?"

"He just wasn't!"

"But why not?"

"How many times do you want me to say it?"

"I asked you a question, and I'd like an answer."

"Then I'll repeat myself one last time: If he wanted

to be a father, he shouldn't have come all the way out here to earn money."

The guy from Guizhou's bizarre logic threw everyone into confusion. The police could only ask him over and over, but the answer was always the same, down to his phrasing. He simply had a weird way of looking at the question.

There were way too many fights, and plenty of people got killed that way. As long as everything was done properly, it wasn't impossible that families of the two sides might come to an agreement. If they didn't want to go to court, there was private mediation, which basically meant settling on a price. Tianxiu's parents and wife fundamentally objected to the option—they wanted punishment. They believed an evil act deserved retribution and weren't interested in money in return for Tianxiu's life. Rather surprisingly, the Guizhou guy didn't want to go the private route either. He had no money, but even if he'd been loaded, and even though he might have ended up facing the firing squad, he outright refused a settlement. Big Six said, "The dog-fucker's crazy."

What came next was a complicated series of events, and nobody could have rushed through it even if they'd wanted to. The inner workings of the construction company were slow. Baolai and I wound up having to find Tianxiu's family a couple of reasonably priced rooms nearby. They just stared at each other, so broken up they could have dashed their brains out, but the parents felt they had to keep their composure for the widow, and she wanted to do the same for them— neither wanted to trigger a greater sorrow. Whenever they had a free moment, the three of them would go to the public phone where Tianxiu had been beaten to death and sit on the curb for half an hour or so. The chalk outline had faded away, but still they stared at the spot. He was gone, but none of them could say so out loud, afraid of bursting into painful sobs. The heartless one in all this was Yulou. I'd bring him over to play at our pingfang when I had nothing better to do, and as soon as he'd step out their front door, the little guy would be full of happiness, giggling at everything he saw, calling every man taller than five feet "Baba." Hearing him say that word brought tears to my eyes.

Tianxiu's wife was the first to crack. She was so broken-hearted that she could neither eat nor sleep, and she kept having nightmares from which she'd wake in a cold sweat. Her legs trembled when she walked. I took her to the clinic. The old lady working there moonlighted in traditional medicine and felt her pulse before telling her to hurry home to the village: "If you stay here any longer you might lose your life too; you'll just have to accept he's gone, my girl, try to overcome your grief." Tianxiu's wife wept again, clutching the doctor's hands. "It's all my fault. If only I hadn't let him come."

The old lady patted her hand. "If he wanted to go, you couldn't have stopped him; if he wanted to stay, he wouldn't have left. It's the course of nature."

5

A couple of days before they were due to leave, Tianxiu's wife snuck out without telling her in-laws and went to see the guy from Guizhou. The police officers at the station were confused by her request. It was awkward, because no one was supposed to meet with the suspect. Tianxiu's wife didn't care about that. With tears in her eyes, she said, "A twenty-five-year-old widow wants to see the man who beat her husband to death. Can't I do that?"

The officer was stunned. "Do you really want to see him?"

"If I don't, I won't have any peace in this lifetime."

"Well, all right then." A twenty-five-year-old widow. The very words sent a chill through their hearts. They decided to bend the rules, just that once.

I went with her to the detention center, carrying her child all the way there. Because I'd taken on the heavy responsibility of protecting this mother and son, I was allowed to enter the room too. Before we went in, she took Yulou from me, insisting on carrying him herself. The room was chilly, and maybe it was just my imagination, but I thought I sensed a sort of lifeless atmosphere. The Guizhou guy was already seated beyond the metal bars, unshaven and jowly, eyes bloodshot from exhaustion. His expression was despairing as he stared at us with dead eyes. Then again, given the surroundings and the feel of the place, no one behind those bars was going to come across as decent. Still, he didn't look quite as vicious as I'd imagined a murderer would. It was just his defiance I found hard to take.

We sat across from him. The guard was worried that Tianxiu's wife would get worked up; he stood right behind her with his hands up, ready to clamp down on her shoulders at any moment. She said nothing, and I had no reason to speak. Yulou looked from his mother to me and instinctively knew to keep his mouth shut too. The Guizhou guy was silent. The atmosphere felt like elastic slowly stretching taut, and with my weak nerves, I could feel the air itself tensing, as if an invisible clock's second hand was madly spinning. A very long time seemed to pass, but we'd been given only three minutes. Those minutes had mostly elapsed when Tianxiu's wife abruptly spoke: "You beat my husband to death."

The Guizhou guy glanced at her, bowed his head, and then raised it again. In a raspy voice, he said, "I'll pay for it with my life."

Yulou turned to look at me, then at the man behind the bars. "Baba!" he said shrilly.

The man from Guizhou almost jumped to his feet. He leaned forward so quickly, his head bumped against the grille.

Again, Yulou cried out, "Baba!"

The Guizhou guy's lips slowly began to tremble. "Son," he said as if talking in his sleep. His eyes grew wet, and the shivering spread to his whole body. He stood abruptly. "I want my son!"

Time was up. The guard told us to leave right away, while another guard escorted the Guizhou guy out. He kept babbling about his son as he moved to the exit.

That night, two middle-aged men came to see Tianxiu's family. One had a Guizhou accent. The other one, who spoke more standard Mandarin, was a lawyer. They were there to convey the Guizhou guy's regret and to pass on a request: He was so sorry to Tianxiu's whole family, to his wife and son, and, if possible, he would do his very best to scrape together an adequate amount of compensation. If he could spend one fewer day in jail, if he could live one more day, that extra day would be suffused with gratitude toward Tianxiu's family. He would burn incense to the Boddhisatva to repent and to comfort Tianxiu's soul in the heavens above. He hoped there would be room for mercy in the trial and sentencing to come. It was a sudden reversal for the Guizhou guy, but the family's response was exactly the same as before: "Hell no!"

The men showed up again the following afternoon, and with them was a director from the construction company where Tianxiu had worked. They wanted a word with the parents alone, so Tianxiu's wife went into the next room to pack. The director suggested they reconsider their position on compensation: There's no bringing the dead back to life, but the living must go on. Even if the two of them were able to eke out an existence, what would come of their daughter-in-law and grandson? Their lives were just beginning, and no one would be able to help them get through all the difficulties they might face. A poor widow and her fatherless child. "It's our responsibility to calmly and pragmatically consider what's best for them. I urge you to rethink your position."

Tianxiu's parents understood perfectly well that

the director's real goal was to reduce the cost to his company, but they had to admit he had a point. They could put the Guizhou guy in front of the firing squad a hundred thousand times, and Tianxiu would still be nothing but ash. They were old, and there was nothing they could do. That afternoon, for the first time ever, Tianxiu's father realized he had no promises he could make his grandson. The old couple sobbed, and the father said, "Tianxiu's our son, but more than that, he was a husband and father. We don't have the right to make this decision."

The visitors were disappointed. Tianxiu's wife appeared in the doorway and said, "What I want to know is, why did he suddenly change his mind?"

The tall man from Guizhou said, "Well, lady, that's just it. So, I'm his cousin. Seeing your kid yesterday caused my cousin to completely change his mind. With all his heart, he knows he's caused you harm. He has deprived a little boy of his father. He's a father too, and his son's gone now—his wife took him away to live with someone else."

"Is he fit to be a father?" Tianxiu's wife said, weeping again. "He's a father himself, and he couldn't wait one minute for our Tianxiu to hear Yulou call him Baba?"

"Please, have a seat." The unassuming man from Guizhou stood, offering his chair to her. "You've got it right again, ma'am. But I haven't had a chance to explain to you—my cousin is actually a good person."

What the Guizhou man meant was that his cousin was a decent guy; he was just having trouble being away from home. All the proper men in their village had left for the city, where there was money to be made, and he had been the only one still hanging around. But how could he have earned a living staying home? His wife was furious and kept quarreling with him. They considered themselves husband and wife—they had a child, after all—but they didn't actually have a marriage certificate. His wife took their son into town, where she sometimes did a bit of trading, and threatened to not come home again if he didn't go to the city. Time went by, and a man in town took a shine to her, a man with quite a bit of money. She phoned their neighbor and asked to speak to her husband: "I'll give you one minute," she said, "to decide if you're leaving or if you're going to stay home." He said nothing, and a minute later the line went dead. Even if he'd wanted to, he couldn't have forced the words out. A couple of days after that, word arrived that his wife had gotten a marriage certificate with that other guy.

Tianxiu's boss was absorbed in the story too. Leaning forward, he asked, "And the kid?"

"Gone with the wife, of course," said the tall Guizhou man. "My cousin had no money, and no tits either; how was he supposed to raise a kid?"

The day his girlfriend was due to marry another man, the guy who beat Tianxiu to death had gone to the county town and bought a train ticket to Beijing. He'd begun having frequent nightmares in which that one minute on the phone took on solid form, a gigantic meteorite that kept shifting shape, dropping from the sky onto his courtyard, smashing his house to pieces with an enormous crash, flinging his son away like a stone from a slingshot. At the construction site on the western edge of Beijing, he'd get up in the middle of the night, throw on some clothes, and go out to smoke by the fence. Whenever a co-worker came outside to piss, he'd say to them, "I'm not fit to be a father."

6

The upshot was this: the guy from Guizhou gave Tianxiu's family 180,000 yuan and was sentenced to twenty years in prison. He thanked Tianxiu's parents over and over, wishing Tianxiu's son a happy life.

Oh, and there was the sketchbook.

I went with Tianxiu's parents to the construction site to collect his things. Besides the bare essentials of clothes and toiletries, there was a pile of books and magazines in a cardboard box. The books were too heavy for the old people to carry back to Huajie, and it would have made them sad to hold onto their late son's possessions, so they decided to leave them all at my place for safekeeping. Once the dust had settled, I saw them off at the train station, and then I went home and slowly flipped through the books. Between two magazines I found an old exercise book—the sort every schoolkid had years ago. The pages were covered in drawings: buildings, streets, pedestrians, cars, university gates, parks full of trees. Mostly buildings, though. Even in those simple outlines, you could sense Tianxiu's prowess at geometry, in both two and three dimensions. Some of the diagrams were even annotated with the relevant math. At the top of each page was the date and place. I copied the information into a table, so I could see it all at a glance: On this day, Tianxiu had gone to such-and-such city, then on that day, he moved on.

WHEELS

TURN

Wheels Turn

There was nothing in the world Xian Mingliang couldn't dismiss with this single phrase: Wheels turn. "Wheels turn, so just forget about it." "It has to be this way; wheels keep turning, after all." "All right, let's do it that way: Wheels turn." "You just do what you please; no matter what, wheels keep turning." "That wheel there? Fixed it. Wheels are meant to turn."

Suffice it to say, he never stopped saying "Wheels turn"; it was his catchphrase, the way some people never speak without first uttering a drawn-out "Uhhhh…": usually unnecessary, often quite meaningless. Wheels. Wheels. Wheels wheels wheels. Xian Mingliang loved driving.

He was already a driver when I met him, as a boy growing up in Zhejiang Province. Back then, most of the men in Huajie village were either in trucking or shipping, including those who had married into the neighborhood. When he was twenty-four, he married in from Heding, downriver, becoming the son-in-law of a boat owner, Huang Zengbao. Huang's daughter had been married before, and she had a two-year-old girl, but her husband had died while working on

Huang's boat. It was a bizarre death. He'd been standing in the prow of the boat, smoking, when Huang
called him below deck to eat. He'd turned his head and
then just toppled into the water like a wooden post.
When they dredged him up, his body was cold. That
first husband had married into the family, too. Huang
had been good to him and had planned to leave him
the boat when he was ready to retire. But fate had
other plans: The 85-kilo brute just turned his head
and then died, with no room for argument. Huang had
only his one daughter, and he was determined to have
a son-in-law to carry on the family business, taking
over the boat that Huang had worked his whole life
for. He couldn't imagine leaving it to someone who
wasn't kin. Xian Mingliang had come to Huajie to be
a trucker, and he accompanied an old driver named
Chen Zigui everywhere he went. On long hauls he
would drive and let Chen Zigui nap, slumped over in
the passenger seat. He loved the feeling of operating
those big Liberation-brand trucks all by himself.

When he wasn't behind the wheel, Xian Mingliang
seemed to deflate, and he moped around with his hands
in pockets like a morose slacker. He always wore the
same style of black slacks—loose in the rear, suddenly
narrowing at the calf—and let them ride low on his
hips. Every time I saw him, I felt like they were about
to fall down and wanted to hike them up for him. He
would greet absolutely everyone in Huajie, and he
asked every kid the same question: "Hey, little guy, do
you know what wheels are for?" He was addicted to
this tedious little game. If the kid answered right, he
would give him a piece of candy. If the kid didn't know,

he'd give him the candy anyway. One day, as he was playing with Huang's two-year-old granddaughter, holding out a piece of candy and asking what wheels do, a fortune teller arrived from the east.

In those days plenty of fortune tellers roamed from town to town—they said the blind ones had true vision. But that fortune teller wasn't blind. He couldn't have been: Besides telling fortunes he also read bones, faces, and palms. A crowd immediately gathered from all around—the village was home to plenty of industrious folk, but even more slackers. As a demonstration of his abilities, the fortune teller tugged his goatee (the standard facial hair of nearly all fortune tellers) and read the faces of a few people he picked out of the crowd. Twisty Meng had a mealy face...he probably sold rice. Lan with the pockmarks—though his face was a wreck, his gaze was calm and a little weak... he was probably a tofu maker. Ma Banye had a fierce look, like he knew how to use his fists...he was surely a butcher. Dan Feng... He looked her over and considered his words for a long time before speaking. She would eventually find a man she could rely on. He could tell at a glance that her trade was opening her door to men at midnight.

Many in Huajie had traveled extensively and knew that fortune tellers often had no skills at all. They simply asked around ahead of time and then used that knowledge to deceive their listeners. Once they'd gained some trust, they spun yarns, making stuff up, and the money came rolling in. Someone pointed at Xian Mingliang and asked the fortune teller to read him—he came from Heding, so they figured the fortune teller couldn't have found out about him in advance.

The fortune teller took two turns around Xian Mingliang and Huang's two-year-old granddaughter, then tugged his goatee and said, "Something's not right here. This young man is plainly unmarried, yet this girl is his daughter…though not by birth. Their connection is cloudy to me."

Everyone laughed and began to disperse. Xian Mingliang? Connected to Huang's family? Crazy. They'd caught the fortune teller after all. But just at that moment, Huang's daughter stepped outside to throw out the laundry water, and the fortune teller suddenly pointed at her. "Those two are a couple!"

Everyone laughed even harder, and someone said to Xian Mingliang, "Why don't you help your wife throw out the water?"

The blush on Xian Mingliang's face spread all the way down to his navel, but, laughing weakly, he said in his deflated way, "I'll help her if she agrees to be my wife. You can't tell me wheels don't turn."

"Do you see? They will be husband and wife!" The fortune teller slung his pack on his back and prepared to move on. "If they're not together the next time I pass through, you can dig out my eyes and fry them like quail eggs."

Three months later the fortune teller returned, just ten days after Xian Mingliang moved in with the Huang family—all because of the fortune. After Huang had come in from the river and heard what happened, he invited Xian Mingliang over, and they'd settled things on the spot. Xian Mingliang's only family was a stepfather back in Heding, so he was able to make this momentous decision all on his own. So what if he was marrying into his wife's family, instead of bringing a wife into his own? He was still a man, and now a father, too. The fortune teller did a spanking business after that. He held court in a tavern by the canal docks, and people came from Flower Street, East Street, West Street, and South Street, cash in hand, wanting their fortunes told. My own grandfather had his face read and learned that his visage bespoke great fortune and that a great talent would be born among his children's children. I had just started elementary school, and my grades really were quite good. My grandfather asked him if I would attend university. "He won't stop there!" said the fortune teller. My grandfather was beside himself. The price was 150 yuan, but he gave 200.

A few years later I moved to Beijing, though not to attend college as the fortune teller had predicted. It was in my junior year of high school, when I was seventeen, that I withdrew from school because of my weak nerves. I couldn't concentrate on my books, couldn't sleep, and all day long my head felt like it was being squeezed by a band of iron. If I'd stayed in school, I would have gone crazy. All my classmates were knuckling down, trying to edge their way through the door, while I could only wander through the schoolyard like a lost spirit, an outsider, a nervous wreck. One day I found a secluded place and broke down and cried, then I returned to my dorm, collected my things, and went home. I told my family I'd rather die than stay in that school. I was done. My father couldn't understand how my perfectly ordinary-looking head had gone so wrong. "All right then," he said, "it's the easy route you're after, right? Go with your uncle to Beijing and help him with his work. Earn yourself a little money, and give that strange head of yours a rest." So, that's how I ended up following Thirty Thou Hong to Beijing and settling down in a pingfang on the western outskirts of Beijing. We really were on the outskirts—we were practically in the countryside. When we weren't working in the city itself, the only way I could see it was by climbing onto the roof and looking east: Beijing was a tropical rainforest made up of endless tall buildings and the glow of neon lights.

I spent my nights pasting little advertisements everywhere for my uncle's fake ID business. My roommate Baolai and I were responsible for disseminating his phone number as widely as possible throughout the city. Baolai was a bit older than me and had been doing it for a while; we slept in the same room, in bunk beds. There was another set of bunk beds in the room, too, where Xingjian and Miluo slept. They pasted advertisements for a different maker of fake IDs, Chen Xingduo, and were both a little older than me.

"Yup, wheels keep turning, goddamn it."

I heard a voice speak those words, and after so many years my ears still twitched. I was eating dinner with Baolai at the donkey-burger place near where we lived. No one else would ever say anything like that—even the deflated tone of voice sounded familiar. I turned to see Mingliang sitting at another table with a fat man with stained, oily hands. Mingliang was sporting a side-part hairdo and wearing jeans instead of his old black slacks. The cuffs of his jeans were frayed at the back from being stepped on, so I guessed he still wore them low on his hips. The right side of his mouth twisted in a grin—he looked drunk. As he propped his left leg up on a stool, he caught sight of me and Baolai. "Oh, you two!" he said as he stood up and came over to us.

The fat man with oily hands said, "So, Mingliang, we have a deal?"

Xian Mingliang flapped a hand and said, "I said wheels turn, didn't I? You've just got to treat my two young friends here to dinner."

"No problem."

Mingliang wanted a job in the fat man's car repair garage, and after four bottles of beer, six donkey burgers, and three plates of garlic cucumber they'd come to an agreement. Mingliang was a skilled worker and wasn't asking much. When he first arrived in Beijing, he'd worked for a maker of fake IDs, and his specialty had been making fake driver's licenses, but he'd made only forty of them before his boss was caught. That was the thing about this line of work—you could go down at any time. Lucky for Mingliang he was a fast runner, or he probably would have been nabbed too. He'd gone hungry for two days before coming across the owner of the garage.

Prior to coming to Beijing, he'd been in jail for four years. He'd run someone over with his truck.

After getting married, his new father-in-law,

Huang, insisted that he switch professions. After two years of an apprenticeship, he'd be able to run his own boat. Then Huang could finally retire and bounce his granddaughter on his knee. A grandson would be even better—he was counting on Xian Mingliang. But Xian Mingliang wouldn't listen—it was the only way in which he disobeyed Huang. The people in Huajie thought highly of Xian Mingliang, saying even a natural-born son wouldn't be so considerate and that Huang had done well, but he still refused to change professions, because he'd wanted to be a driver ever since he was small. Even when he didn't have a car, he'd ride a bike or drive a tractor and would help people fix up their tractors for free. He eventually decided to throw his lot in with the old driver Chen Zigui and finally became a driver himself, and he continued to tell everyone he saw about how wheels were meant to turn.

"I can't be bothered to argue with people," he said with a smile when asked why he was so accommodating to people. "I just do what they say. Nobody's ever asked me to commit murder or arson; why should I stress it? I'm fine so long as I can drive my truck—wheels turn, right?"

His marriage was happy, or at least it looked that way. He was very good to his abruptly acquired two-year-old daughter and would always bring her back treats from his long hauls. The girl called him "Baba" as though he were her real father. But just when everyone had started thinking of him as a village native, everything changed.

Given his skill as a driver, the accident could only have

happened at night, at a fork in the road, and when he'd been drinking. At dusk, as he passed through the town of Tianchang in Anhui Province, a breeze carried a sweet scent into the cab of his truck. It was a beautiful evening, and his truck seemed to fly. The colors of the evening rose from the earth like drops of ink soaking up through paper, and the whole world began to sink into black and gray. "There's nothing as relaxing as driving at that time of day." Even now Mingliang thinks back fondly on the sunset that evening. "Then I got to the fork. Why must wheels turn?" His face changes here whenever he tells the story; his lips tremble. Then it was truly dark. A bicycle hurtled out of the righthand side of the fork, and *bang*—by the time he braked, he'd rolled right over it.

Mingliang got out of his truck and heard someone crying out; he knew immediately he'd been in an accident. He'd never in his life imagined he'd have an accident. Five meters behind the truck, a man was lying next to his bicycle; both were misshapen. The bike's rear wheel was still spinning, feebly. The man spoke, in agony: "Put me out of my misery."

"I'll take you to the hospital," said Mingliang, shaking from head to toe.

"No, just kill me…"

Mingliang thought he'd misheard. He steeled himself and approached the man. He was handicapped; there was a wooden crutch nearby—it was hard to imagine how he'd ever gotten on the bicycle. But now he was certainly paralyzed; the truck had crushed both of his thighs.

"I'll take you to the hospital."

"No. Look at me." He spoke haltingly. Though he wanted to die, he could hardly stand the pain. "I waited for you at this fork for a long time. Just back up the truck; you'll be doing me a favor." Then he began to beg.

Mingliang, scared out of his wits, agreed. "He was asking me for help, I had to do it. As I backed up my whole body shook, from the inside out, and I was covered in cold sweat—even my fingernails and toenails were sweating. You have to believe me: Wheels keep turning no matter what. I backed the truck up five meters, six, seven, and I heard a great cry, a sort of cry of joy. I kept backing up until the front wheels went over him as well. I don't know why he insisted on dying, but he wanted it so badly I had to help. Then I stopped the truck and sat by the road, completely soaked in sweat, waiting for the next car to come by. Ten minutes later a motorcycle appeared; I gave the driver ten yuan and told him, "Do me a favor, brother. Find a phone and call the police; tell them I'm waiting here."

He told them everything, but the cops didn't believe him—they believed him even less when they found he'd been drinking. It was hopeless; they would do what they needed to do. However you looked at it, he'd run someone over. In court he was asked, "Do you confess?"

He said, "You won't believe me, so I guess I have to confess. Wheels turn."

"What did you say?" they asked.

"I said wheels turn. That's for sure."

"He's crazy," they said. "Put him away!"

After he'd done four of his five years, they let him out

for good behavior. He couldn't say whether his behavior was really good or not—he just did whatever they told him and spent the rest of the time napping against the wall. When he was awake, he imagined his truck, stripping it down from the whole to its parts and then back to its whole again, mulling endlessly over every piece. In the last year he was given the opportunity to look after the prison vehicles; that was when he was happiest. In order to spend as much time as possible with the vehicles, he would break a little something here even as he fixed a little something there; that way he could go from vehicle to vehicle, as though it were a regular job. When he had no cars or trucks to fix, he still enjoyed fixing wheelbarrows. When he got out of the prison the officials praised him as a good worker.

When he returned to Huajie he found that things had changed—his wife now had a one-year-old boy. He could have ignored it if the little guy were three or four, but he was only one. But when you got right down to it, wheels were still turning, and there was nothing that couldn't be explained—if there was something you couldn't make sense of, it was because you didn't want to make sense of it. Mingliang didn't want to think about it, but of course he understood. Huang sat, smoking silently with a hired boat-hand in the other room. Huang's daughter sat across from Mingliang, holding her year-old son, and said, "If you don't want to accept this son, we can get divorced."

Mingliang rubbed his bald head. "Do you want me to accept him, or do you want to get divorced?"

"It's up to you."

"That means you want a divorce." He stood up and

walked into the yard, calling into the other room: "I'm leaving; you can have them."

The smoking boat-hand coughed once, almost an expression of gratitude, and dropped his unused knife on the ground.

After the accident and his time in jail, Mingliang couldn't find any work as a driver back home—no one would have him. Even Chen Zigui's appeals on his behalf did no good. Driving was a superstitious profession. It was unlucky to drive over clothing in the road, and you really had to steer around dead cats and dogs. Getting into an accident that resulted in a person dying was most unlucky of all. In the donkey-burger joint, I examined Mingliang's new look: He'd exchanged his shaved head for a part, but clearly his hair was the only thing he paid any attention to. He'd let his hair grow long just so that he would have to look at himself in the mirror when he brushed it in the morning. A buddy in jail had told him that: You've got to look at yourself in the mirror every day; you've got to think about what you want. You can't just muddle through the days.

"So, Mingliang," asked Baolai. "Do you know what you want?"

"If I did, I'd shave my head again and quit looking in the mirror."

"You need wheels to turn," I said.

"My ass," said Xian Mingliang. "Don't you know wheels are *already* turning?"

I wasn't sure if I knew that or not. Just saying "wheels turn" didn't mean I knew it for a fact.

Xian Mingliang had nowhere to sleep that night and wanted to stay with us. That was fine with me—I'd give him my bed and squeeze in with Baolai. Baolai was fat, but I was skinny. I wasn't more than forty-five kilos soaking wet.

We drank too much beer. Just before dawn, Mingliang woke with a bursting bladder, and as he headed for the bathroom, he saw Baolai and me sitting on the top bunk like sages on the mountaintop. Not only that, but Xingjian and Miluo were lying awake in their beds as well. "What are you all doing?" he asked. "Group meditation?"

"We can't sleep," I said.

"Someone's been setting off fireworks!" said Xingjian, turning over.

"Fireworks? Little punk! If my snoring annoys you just wake me up; wheels turn, right? Anyway, the sun's almost up," he said, getting dressed. "I'm going out for a stroll; you can go back to sleep."

"The sun's almost up," said Baolai. "No one's sleeping."

"Whatever. Just don't blame me for interrupting your sweet dreams."

By that point we really didn't care if we slept more or not. We mostly pasted our ads at night, and we often didn't get to bed until sun-up anyway; we'd only knocked off early the night before because Mingliang was staying with us. He came back from the toilet and told us that we all ought to learn to snore—the louder the better. He'd learned it inside, where, if you didn't snore, then forget about sleeping at night—everyone snored like it was a competition, each louder than the next. Mingliang's snores were out of all proportion to his physique—he ought to have been fifty kilos heavier. "Let's see what you got," he said to us.

Despite that, the next night he went to sleep on the roof. He arranged himself on four chairs under the canopy of the sky, and the following morning he awoke with his head soaked in dew. He'd been expecting to live at the mechanic's garage, but there wasn't room, and the stink of gas was too strong anyway. With the door open the boss worried about burglars, but with it closed he'd be poisoned. He liked cars, but not enough to suffocate. But he couldn't sleep long term in the open air either—when the wind changed to come from the north, Beijing cooled down a lot. It was breezy on the roof. We often sat up there to play Ace of Spades. Whoever drew the ace of spades was the enemy of the other three. You had to keep it close to your chest if you had it. If the others knew you had it, they would gang up to destroy you, and if you were beaten you had to treat everyone to beer and kebabs. Mingliang would join us on the roof when business was slow in the garage and play with us. It was usually Baolai who drew the ace, but Mingliang was drawing it hand after hand, and hand after hand he was ganged up on by the rest of us. Empty bottles from all the beers he treated us to were lined up in ranks along the wall, over which we looked out across Beijing.

A couple of weeks later, Xian Mingliang got his first paycheck, and he rented a little room in the alley to the left of us. The day he moved in, he was too late to buy a sleeping mat, so he spent that night on the bare mattress. He lived simply and enjoyed his work in the garage. He also had a hobby, which was gathering discarded car parts—he said eventually he'd have enough to build his own car. Normally such parts were sold for scrap, and even the small pieces brought in a little cash. His fat boss bemoaned the loss but said, "You can take those, but when customers come you've got to use the best parts on their cars; you've got to earn it back double."

"As long as they follow my recommendations," said Xian Mingliang.

When I went out jogging, I'd often pass by his room. I jogged because my doctor had told me it was the best cure for weak nerves, gradually restoring flexibility to the flaccid nerves. And once they were like elastic bands fresh from the factory again, you were cured. So I jogged every day, imagining my head to be full of elastic bands growing gradually tighter the more I ran. I'd stop at Xian Mingliang's room when he was home. The scrap metal heaped in the corner really was scrap—pitch black and filthy. Maybe it was because of my weak nerves, but I lacked the imagination to see that heap becoming a shiny new car. He had a detailed blueprint in his head, though, and knew precisely where each piece of twisted metal would go.

"Behold, comrades, our mighty capital!" It was after a game of Ace of Spades, and Miluo was gesturing southeast like a great leader. His lyric right arm seemed to extend farther and farther until it became a bird that flew right over Beijing. We young men (even counting me, a high-school dropout) viewed this vast and bustling capital with boundless expectation.

Everyone in the whole country knew this place was full of money—you only had to bend over and pick it up. Everyone in the whole country knew that opportunity here was like birdshit—it would spatter on your head while you weren't looking and make you rich.

From what I'd seen, however, there were fewer and fewer birds in Beijing. The place had once been full of sparrows and crows, but you hardly ever saw them now. They said it was because the glass in the skyscrapers dazzled them and they smashed against the windows. There were still some parrots, thrushes, and magpies but they were mostly in cages, and you couldn't expect them to fly up and shit opportunity on you. In the end, we might be left with just a single bird in the sky: Miluo's lyric right hand, which, no matter what, could never shit on you. But none of that disturbed the sweet dreams of all the young people rushing into Beijing.

Mingliang looked out over Beijing's distant rolling skyline, his gaze soaring like Miluo's right hand then sliding on down to rest on a highway at the far end of the town.

"I'd like a car," he said, dropping into his chair and propping one leg on the other. "If I had all the money in the world, I'd find some empty road and just drive. Just keep driving. Wheels turn, you know."

It was a pretty disappointing dream. Just driving around in some crappy car—what would be the purpose of all that driving?

One evening Xian Mingliang came over and asked us to help him move. His voice was nasal, sounding as though it was coming from Beijing's distant far-eastern suburbs. His nose dripped a clear liquid, and his eyes were red. His room was so packed with spare parts that he'd had to move his bed just outside the door, and after sleeping there for two nights he'd gotten a bad cold. We could hardly imagine how he could sleep outside on such chilly nights, just a skyful of stars hanging over him. I felt his blanket—it seemed like a firm squeeze would wring water out of it. The five of us could only worm our way into the cracks and gaps of the six-square-meter room. The scrap metal really was just junk, though he'd arranged it convincingly (we didn't recognize any of it, of course, but getting all those bits and pieces in one place counted for something)—filthy and black, it wasn't very confidence inspiring. We nearly exhausted ourselves moving the whole pile out under the eaves, then helping him bring his bed and an old table back inside. These two jobs done, we put up a little shack under the eaves to cover the car guts—Mingliang didn't want them exposed to the wind and sun and rain. He knew exactly he was doing with this incomprehensible pile. "Just wait," he said. "When it's done, I'll take you out for a spin; you can't tell me wheels aren't turning."

A week later, he called us: the car engine was gradually taking shape and needed to be moved to the garage, where it'd eventually be paired with a chassis and wheels. We borrowed a cart from the old grocer next door and made two creaking, straining trips. The fat boss wasn't happy to have so many slackers hanging around his garage, but Mingliang gave him a cigarette and explained that we were all buddies from the same street, and, despite it looking like we'd steal, we were all clean. "What the fuck is *that*?" asked Xingjian.

In the garage was a half-made car body welded together out of rusty metal sheeting, little droplets of metal sticking together the seams. There were wheels, too, four of them, apparently of two different sizes. Mingliang said he hadn't been able to find four identical wheels, and it was a miracle that he'd found the two matching pairs. I thought about how, if he hadn't been able to find the two pairs, he could have just started by making a three-wheeled car. A three-wheeled car is still a car, and wheels turn. I couldn't imagine a three-wheeler driving along Beijing's thoroughfares— perhaps it would be like Neanderthals appearing in Huajie village?

After that, Mingliang had more good news for us each time he came to the roof to play Ace of Spades: "Almost there!" We were waiting for the day he'd drive himself over. And one weekend, after Mingliang got off work, he really did. Scared the crap out of us. I can say with confidence that no more than a handful of human beings have ever laid eyes on a car like that one: It was a monster. Its skin was rusted sheeting—I mean not a speck of paint—which was all he could afford. Besides that, there wasn't even enough of it to go around: He'd been obliged to make a convertible. The rusted convertible was covered in bright patches where he'd ground down the metal droplets from the welded seams. Only those polished patches gleamed under the sun. Leaving aside the wretched seating, scavenged from other people's castoffs, the major problem seemed to be that the front wheels were a lot smaller than the back wheels, and the whole car lunged forward angrily.

"Get in!" said Mingliang. "You've never seen wheels turn like this!"

We got in and took a spin through the local alleys— it would have been dangerous to go on the main roads without a license plate. It wasn't too strange, mostly like any other car, apart from the way it tilted: I had to brace my feet against the legs of the seat in front of me to keep from sliding forward. "That's fixable: Just raise the seat." The license plate could also be resolved. I would ask Thirty Thou Hong to make a fake one, and it wouldn't cost more than a few bottles of beer. Two days later everything was sorted out, and we decided to try the main roads.

It had horsepower, just like Mingliang had said. It made a lot of noise, but it certainly moved. The low front and high back made it seem like it was even more raring to go, like it couldn't be stopped. He'd used the best materials he could find in the trash on this car. At night in the countryside beyond the suburbs there weren't many cars, and they drove fast, but we overtook them all. We howled as we passed each one—the cold wind swept over the open car, and we had to do something to keep ourselves warm. The drivers we passed could only gaze in despair after our fake license plate. Then, somewhere in Mentougou District, the engine stalled, and we were stranded in the wilds.

Xinjian and the others got out and opened the last two bottles of beer while I held the light for Mingliang as he worked out what had gone wrong. As the beer cooled us off, we started feeling the chill. Mingliang fiddled with every part he could think of, but the car remained a pile of metal, even colder than we were. Quickly our main priority became getting warm, so Mingliang gave up and told us to collect dry grass, branches, and bricks from the side of the road. He pulled a little gas from the tank and lit the branches, and we baked the bricks. Around the time that both we and the bricks started to warm up, he suddenly slapped his forehead, reached behind the steering wheel (formerly from a Honda), fixed something, and the engine turned over.

"Goddamn it!" he yelled. "Wheels turn!"

He showed us how to wrap the hot rocks in newspaper and hold them in our laps to keep warm—one of the survival tactics he'd learned as a truck driver. Restored to roaring life, the car leaped forward as if desperate to get out of there.

"Let's name this thing!" said Baolai.

Xinjiang said, "Iron Horse!"

Miluo suggested, "Land Tiger!"

I said, "Stallion!"

"'Stallion' it is," said Xian Mingliang. "Wheels keep turning!"

We hadn't anticipated the reception "Stallion" would get: Within ten days, it was the mascot of the boss's garage. Parked outside, it was a constant advertisement, less a car than a piece of rough-hewn art. What skills this mechanic must have, to create such a powerful, mad-looking machine out of abandoned parts! The fat boss was happy at first but grew less so: Mingliang often parked the car in his own alley, and when customers who'd heard about it and come to the garage to gawk—and hopefully buy some spare parts and get some repairs done—saw nothing outside, they simply sped away.

"You've got to leave that car outside the garage," said the boss.

"I suppose I could," said Mingliang. "But I'm worried someone will mess with it, and that fake license plate isn't going to hold up forever."

"You've got to."

"All right, I will. I can't help wheels turning."

The garage was about a twenty-minute walk from where Mingliang lived, a walk he'd never minded before, but now that he had the Stallion it seemed awfully far. Worse, any time it started to rain or blow, he had to run over and put a rain cover on it. He wanted to buy some car sheeting and cover it up at the end of each workday—the money could come out of his salary. But the boss glared at him—what was the difference between covering it up and just driving it away? If he wanted to cover it, he could cover only the steering wheel and dashboard. That was infuriating, but Mingliang had no choice—wherever the Stallion was, he wanted it to be protected as much as possible from the wind and rain.

But that wasn't the end of it: Some meddling bastard came to the boss wanting to buy it. He thought it was cool, that it had personality: the perfect combination of artistry and practicality. "Sure, it's cool," the guy said. "But it's the roughness I like. I'll make you an offer." The boss revealed the exact offer to no one, but it was enough to buy a brand-new Toyota. The guy had also noted that scrap metal by itself was worthless, but once made into something like this...

The boss brought Mingliang to the donkey-burger place and ordered four bottles of beer, four donkey burgers, and a plate of five-spice donkey meat. "There's something we've got to discuss," he said. Mingliang drank the beer and ate the meat. "What's on your mind? Either way, wheels turn."

"Just leave the car with me outside the garage, and I'll give you a raise."

"No, I made it in my spare time."

"I'll triple your salary," said the boss, opening the fourth bottle of beer, "and the car does belong to the garage."

"You want it?"

"That's not what I'm saying. It will belong to the garage. And the garage belongs to all of us."

"It already does belong to the garage."

"Well, just sign here, then." The boss pulled a piece of paper out of his pants pocket. At the top was written "Deed of Transfer." He'd already signed under his own name.

Mingliang said it was the first time in his life he'd just walked out on someone. He stood, called for the bill, dropped thirty yuan on the table, and left. He came to our place to finish his dinner. His luck was bad; he was caught with the Ace of Spades and had to pay for four bottles of beer. At the time we had no idea that there had been an offer for Stallion—we were just pissed at how he'd been treated. "Our Xian Mingliang grubbed in the trash each night, putting it together screw by screw, and you just want to take it away?" we wanted to say to the boss. "You think you're the government or something?"

Xingjian said, "Listen to me, brother: Keep your eye on that thing. Wheels are turning, right?"

"Yup," said Mingliang. "Wheels are turning. All I wanted was a car. Even one as rundown as this. Why is that so hard?"

The next day he came back, saying, "He said I used his tools and electricity."

"What did you say?" we asked.

"I said I could pay him."

The day after he returned again, saying, "He said I got a fake license plate; that's illegal."

"What did you say?" we asked.

"I said I could get a real one."

"And then?"

"He said I'd already broken the law. And I've got a record—if they take me in again, I'll never get out. Goddamn, wheels turn."

The day after that he came over again, saying, "Today a police officer came to the garage and walked around the Stallion three times. He asked me where I was from, about my family, and whether life was good in Beijing."

"What did you say?" we asked.

"I said my stepfather died, and I had no family. I said as long as I could see that car outside, I thought life in Beijing was pretty good."

That day he played Ace of Spades with us on the roof until it was so dark we couldn't see the cards in our hands. He treated us to beer, donkey burgers, and five-spice donkey meat. As the sky darkened, we couldn't see his expression anymore and didn't bother to look too closely; we all had good hands and were fidgeting in our haste to catch the Ace. The five-spice donkey meat was excellent, too, with donkey heart, liver, lungs, tripe, and everything.

A couple of days later, we heard that something had happened to Mingliang. Something had happened to his fat boss, too. They were going to make a booze delivery to the Zhang family at the foot of the Fragrant Hills, and Mingliang asked if he could drive them in the Stallion. He drove fast—it was the Stallion, after all—and as he was making a left turn, the left front wheel fell off. His boss, sitting in the passenger seat, flew out of the car, which flipped over a few times. The remaining three wheels spun against the evening sky. The boss went headfirst into a tree trunk, which pushed his head right down into his chest—it took the morticians forever to pull it out again.

The four of us went to visit Xian Mingliang in the hospital, where he lay with four broken ribs. His head was wrapped in an enormous bandage, and his left arm was broken. Miluo—who'd long ago resolved never to drive a car as long as he lived—timidly asked the question we were all curious about: Why hadn't the boss been wearing his seat belt?

"Is there a seat belt on the passenger side?" asked Xian Mingliang with some difficulty. "I don't think I ever installed one there."

Miluo wondered if he was remembering wrong. When he'd sat there the last time, hadn't Xian Mingliang insisted he fasten his seatbelt?

"Did they find the wheel?" Every time he spoke, four ribs hurt.

"They did," I told him. "It rolled into the dry grass at the side of the road. Don't worry, it didn't lose its shape—it'll still turn."

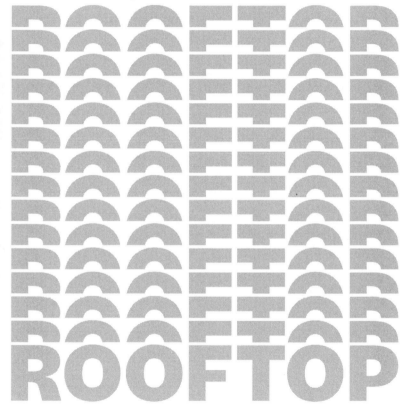

ON THE
ROOFTOP

On the Rooftop

My head throbbed and I felt a bright bird bursting from it. Having broken its metallic body free, it flapped its wings harder and harder, gleaming silver in the late afternoon sun. If it flew to the west, it would see private homes, undeveloped land, the stark fifth and sixth ring roads, the western hills, over whose peaks it would disappear. If it headed east, there'd be nothing but apartments and streets, buildings like mountains and avenues like valleys, people and vehicles flowing thickly down them. To the bird, Beijing must have seemed infinitely vast, so enormous you couldn't catch your breath. Glinting in the light, it flew on and on.

"Hey, play a card!"

I tossed one down. "Bird."

They stared at me, eyes wide.

I hastily corrected myself. "Six of clubs, I mean."

"Yeah, maybe that looks like a cock, not a bird."

We were on the rooftop playing Ace of Spades, shrouded by the shade of the pagoda tree. In our basic single-story pingfang on the outskirts of Haidian District on the western edge of Beijing, from summer to fall, we spent our days playing cards on that roof.

Since moving in, on warm days I followed my friends'
protruding asses up to the roof, and somehow the ace
of spades always ended up with Baolai. Round after
round, at least ninety-five out of a hundred times. It
got to the point that as soon as the cards were dealt,
one of us would say, "Go on, Baolai, show us the ace."

And he'd obediently produce it. "Here."

It was never surprising when it was another
loss for him. When he'd give me my winnings—a
Zhongnanhai cigarette and a glass of Yanjing beer—
I'd push them back at him. "Let the others have this,
Baolai."

I felt a bit sorry for him. I neither smoked nor
drank, and I felt awkward with a cigarette between my
lips and a beer in my hand. I'd moved to Beijing at
the start of the summer after dropping out of school
from what the doctor told me were "weak nerves."
He'd written me a prescription without much fuss:
nerve and brain tonic, a solution of vitamins and
sodium phosphate. Every time I felt my brain tighten
or my head throb, I'd take a swig. It came in a can that
looked like DDT, and every time I pulled off the lid,
I'd imagine it was poison. Its therapeutic effects were
negligible. Around four or five every afternoon, I stood
atop the second-year school block, facing the sun, still
feeling that inexplicable panic, as if the whole world
were filled with the violent thudding of my heart, and
my every vein would thrum. The doctor called them
"palpitations." Fine, but why was I palpitating? The
Monkey King's cursed metal band tightened around
my head whenever I tried to read. The headaches
meant I couldn't sleep, and then I wouldn't wake up

on time the next morning. Even if I did manage to drift off, I only wafted along the surface of sleep and would jolt awake at so much as a mosquito's sneeze. I often saw another me standing by my bedside staring, while the other seven guys in my dorm happily snored, ground their teeth, talked in their sleep, and farted. The doctor had said, "Go jogging; that'll help stimulate your nerves. Did you know that when your nerves are too tense, they lose their elasticity? Like a worn-out rubber band. You have to train and train and train, until your nerves regain their resilience." But it wasn't like I could climb out of bed in the middle of the night and go running.

The doctor kept saying, "Run." So I packed up my stuff and headed home, abandoning my studies. I told my parents they could beat me to death, but I wasn't going back. They were perplexed by my strange illness. My baba circled me, right hand raised, thumb and index finger poised to find and pluck the gleaming metal thread from my head. *Don't let it get away. Where are you, you son of a bitch?* He found nothing, nothing at all. Eventually he slumped on the old rattan chair whose legs were all different lengths and said dejectedly to Ma, "Well, he's got nothing better to do; why don't we send him to Beijing with Thirty Thou? If he's lucky, he might earn a bit of beer money."

"He's only seventeen," said Ma.

"So what? My baba was seventeen when I was born!"

So that's how I ended up going to Beijing with Thirty Thou Hong, my uncle who sold fake IDs in the city. From the way he dressed and the cigarette clamped between his lips, you knew he'd made it big. He only smoked Zhongnanhai Point-Eights. He generously gave a whole carton to his relatives, and we all got to try them. The leaders of our nation smoked that brand. My baba took two: one to smoke and one to tuck behind his ear. He took it out from time to time just to sniff at. So now here I was, living with Xingjian, Miluo, and Baolai in this pingfang, paying two-forty-a-month rent. We slept in two bunk beds in one room, and all four of us did the same work: going out at night and putting up small ads. You took a Sharpie, found an empty bit of wall somewhere eye catching, and wrote *Seals and Documents Please Contact (510) 939-1493.* Xingjian and Miluo worked for Chen Xingduo, while Baolai and I worked for my uncle. Sometimes we didn't use a pen or paste up ads, but dabbed a carved yam onto an ink-soaked sponge as a stamp. Much faster than writing. I was in charge of carving the words into the root vegetable. You wouldn't call it pretty, but it was legible at a glance.

We worked only at night, to avoid getting arrested. The squinty, watchful eyes of security guards and police officers were everywhere, and they'd nab whomever they could. They'd all be asleep by the small hours, though, even in the wealthy district of Zhongguancun. The two of us boldly wrote and stamped our message on walls, bus stops, overhead bridges, stairs, even on the street itself. Sanitation workers would wash away our words, and we'd rewrite them. Let wildfires burn them down; spring breezes would raise them again. People who wanted seals carved or documents sorted out would obediently follow the trail of breadcrumbs to

Thirty Thou Hong, and he'd pass the job on to his forgers. I wasn't sure how much he actually earned doing this, but he paid us 500 a month. Baolai said, "This isn't bad, bro. We go out after midnight and make our rounds, like taking a nighttime stroll. And we get paid for it!" He was content, and I was too. Not because of the money, but because I liked the night. It was quiet in the early hours, when Beijing's dust had settled. The roads were like dry riverbeds, and the city felt much larger. Nighttime Beijing seemed more spacious, a vast and empty landscape beneath gentle streetlights. Ever since my nerves weakened, my dreams had grown to be as jostling and fragmented as daytime Beijing. If I could have dreamed such a scene of capacious peace as the night, I'd probably have woken out of sheer joy.

We slept from dawn till the afternoon. To make sure I was tired enough, I forced myself to jump around in my spare time and jogged every chance I got. If you happened to be wandering around Beijing back then in the small hours of the night, you might have seen a tall, skinny teenager with spiky hair hyperactively haunting the streets and alleyways of the capital. Yup, that was me. And the guy next to me, a little stockier, a little shorter, was Baolai. He was sluggish, and you might have thought he was slow, but I swear on my weak nerves that my friend Baolai wasn't slow at all. He was a solid guy, and he was kind. The best of all the good people I met in Beijing.

Xingjian and Miluo insisted that he was useless and refused to address him with respect, even though he was older than them. He was left to do all the chores around the house: sweeping the floor, taking out the trash, slicing watermelons, opening beer bottles. If he could have eaten their dinner for them, they'd have ordered him to do that too. Not that they ever had to order him around—Baolai did it all of his own accord. He felt that, as the oldest, he ought to take care of us three. At this moment, for instance, we're still sleeping soundly while he lugs the small dining table and four little stools onto the roof. It's some time before sunset. Our only entertainment is Ace of Spades.

Before I arrived, the other three would climb onto the roof not to play cards, but to gawk at women. From up there, you could clearly see their faces and chests as they walked down the alley. As they passed by, the boys would swivel to stare at their legs and asses. It was cooler on the rooftop, with the wind blowing and the old pagoda tree's expansive shade. When I moved in, four was just the right number for a game of cards. I liked being on the rooftop because you could see farther. The doctor had said standing high up and looking into the distance would be good for my nerves. I felt claustrophobic crammed into our little house. Besides, there were skyscrapers nearby, and even taller skyscrapers beyond them. Even just a little higher, it improved my spirits a tiny bit. Though no matter how I stood on tiptoe and craned my neck, I was still low.

I kept quiet while we played cards—talking too much made my head ache. Baolai didn't say much either, just wrinkled his brow like a philosopher deep in thought. All that thinking didn't do him any good, though; the ace of spades kept finding its way into his hand. He never tried to hide it, and Xingjian and Miluo could tell at a glance who had it anyway. I couldn't bluff either—whenever I was unlucky enough to be it, I'd feel the bands of pressure tighten and would have to tap my head with my middle knuckle. Baolai was always slow to throw out a card, and while they waited, Miluo and Xingjian would talk about women. They were one and two years older than me, respectively, but from the way they behaved, I could tell they were old hands at sex. Their familiarity with every part of a woman's body was so detailed, they could have been scientists. If they happened to have a night off from pasting ads, they would go to some underground screening room to watch a late show. Before I met them, I thought the dirtiest films in the world were Category Three. They told me I hadn't seen anything yet—it was all about "A" films! Did I know what that meant? Porn! To be honest, I had no idea then what they were talking about. They laughed at me, and even harder at Baolai. They said they'd get a bit of money together to pay some vegetable-selling auntie to take our virginities.

I kept my head down, my temples throbbing, and I thought about the girl I'd liked in my last year of school. She'd transferred into our class from some southern town. She had a sharp nose and talked with the tip of her tongue poking out between her teeth. The Mandarin she spoke was different from how any of us sounded, even if we put our tongues between our teeth. One day, around this time of the year, she rolled up the sleeves of her T-shirt, stuck her hands in her pockets, and swaggered through the late-afternoon sunlight behind the school, mimicking me. Her hands pulled her pants taut, and I could clearly see the curves of her butt. Standing there in the classroom, I watched through the window as she turned to smile at me. The sun gilded her ass. That's my earliest romantic memory. After that, whenever the subject of women or love came up, two images flashed through my mind: a sharp nose and a gilded ass not yet at its full roundness. Then I'd feel a searing pain in my heart, my temples would ache, and I'd have to lower my head.

One afternoon last month, after we'd watched from the rooftop as a girl in a short skirt walked through the alley, Miluo ordered me to talk about what I knew of "women." I didn't know what else to say, so I told them about my classmate from two years ago. We'd lost touch. Xingjian and Miluo laughed so hard, they almost fell off the roof.

"*Women*, we said!" they chortled.

The way they saw it, if you weren't talking about sex, you weren't really talking about women. I knew I'd strayed from the subject, but I was fine having some distance between me and women. I was only hoping to get closer to my brain, but it seemed determined to stay far away—hurting so much it didn't feel like it was mine.

"What's your favorite part of a woman, Baolai?" Xingjian asked.

"The face," said Baolai, holding a card. Once he had the ace of spades, the other three of us would barricade him so he couldn't discard it. "I need to see a woman's face before I can trust her."

This made no sense. Seeing someone's face didn't mean you could trust them, did it? Baolai didn't explain, and we assumed he was talking nonsense. When someone's lost that many games, you have to let them be a little illogical from time to time. Baolai was clearly going to lose this round too. I couldn't have given him a chance even if I'd wanted to. Miluo went before me, and Xingjian went after, so they were able to squeeze Baolai. He lost eight cards. Including the four rounds from earlier, and not counting the three empty bottles at our feet, he still had to fork over three more bottles of Yanjing beer and a whole pack of Zhongnanhai Eights.

"I'll go get more beer." Baolai said, putting down his cards.

"No hurry, we can settle up when we're done playing." Xingjian didn't want to stop.

"Xingjian, real talk." Miluo said, bringing a beer to his lips. "If you woke up tomorrow afternoon with money, what would you do?"

"Fuck it. Buy a big house, marry a wife nine years older than me, lounge around in bed all day."

"Why nine years older?" I was confused.

"So she'll have experience," said Miluo. "Little girls don't know anything. You need a woman who knows what she wants."

"Twenty-eight is a good age. I'm getting hard just thinking about it. Twenty-eight, oh god, yeah," Xingjian said.

"If I had money, obviously I'd get a house and wife. Also, I'd take taxis everywhere, even to the toilet. Then I'd get a bunch of people, like you guys, to put up ads for me in the middle of the night. Fuck it, I'd be richer than Chen Xingduo!"

"If you had that much money, why not buy a car?" I asked.

"Don't you know I have no sense of direction? I get dizzy going around the third ring road. If I set off for Fangshan, I might head in the totally opposite direction and end up in Pinggu instead." Tapping Baolai's knee with the beer bottle, Miluo said, "What about you, Baolai?"

"Me?" Baolai's lips compressed into a smile. He stood, hitching up his trousers. "I should go get some beer."

"Let's finish talking first."

"I'll be quick." Baolai glanced at his watch. "I'll be back before you've smoked a cigarette."

"What about you, kid?" Xingjian jabbed a finger at me. "Say you had 500 grand."

Five hundred thousand yuan was an astronomical sum to me. I couldn't think how I would spend it. Build a house for my sixty-year-old grandpa and grandma to live out their twilight years? Buy my ba a truckload of Zhongnanhai Eights? Pay to replace my ma's decayed teeth with porcelain crowns, then dye every strand of her prematurely white hair black again? For myself, if anyone could treat my weak nerves, I'd give him all of it.

"Hey, say something," the two of them badgered me. "Would you try to get that classmate of yours?"

Sharp nose, curvy ass. My heart twinged. "I'll help Baolai with the beer." I clambered down after him.

Xingjian and Miluo chorused, "Fun-sucking motherfucker."

They'd gotten to Beijing half a year before me and picked up a few more Beijing swears.

*

The closest convenience store was to our west, but Baolai was heading east. I asked if he was going the wrong way, and he told me to hurry up—we'd jog, which would be good for my nerves. I ran alongside him, down an alley, around a corner. He slowed down in front of Blossoms Bar. The bar couldn't seem to make up its mind about its décor: a bit Tibetan, a bit European, with some cartoon characters and scarecrows thrown in. A rotating pole by the entrance made it look like a barber shop. I'd been inside once, when my uncle Thirty Thou Hong was buying. He ordered me a glass of beer and told me if I didn't step into a bar at least once, I hadn't really been to the big city, and if I didn't have a drink, I hadn't really been inside a bar. The beer had tasted so-so, and I didn't see what was so great about drinking it in a bar. When we'd left, Thirty Thou Hong had called my aunt and then my ba, loudly braying that we'd just been to a bar for a drink, and wasn't that something…

Baolai looked at his watch, asking, "Is it six o'clock yet?"

"One minute to."

"Let's keep running."

I followed him another block, then we turned back. Jogging always helped my head feel less painfully tight. We were back outside Blossoms Bar.

"And now?"

"Nine minutes past six."

"Let me catch my breath."

Baolai sat on some rubble at the foot of a utility pole kitty corner to the bar. Bigger people often sweat a lot, even if they're just a little fat. Baolai fanned his chin. The pole was covered with ads that promised to cure sexually transmitted diseases, body odor, vitiligo, sleepwalking, and prostate cancer, all from unlicensed doctors claiming to be descended from imperial court physicians. I read all the ones I could see, then it was twenty past and I said we should go get the beer. Baolai said "Fine," and then insisted on going to the supermarket to our west, since we were now nearby. He was talking complete garbage—it was at least 350 meters away. When we were done, we left the supermarket and walked past the bar yet again. I snapped. "Man, why're we just going round and round in circles? Like a couple of beetles or something."

"I just want to look." Baolai's face was blazing red. "Guess what I'd do if I made big money?"

I shook my head. For years now, I'd given no thought to any goal other than getting into college.

"I'd open a bar. A place like Blossoms. People would be able to write anything they like on the walls."

I remembered that the walls of Blossoms Bar were complete chaos, covered in words and pictures in all colors. It was the only bar I'd ever set foot in, but I'd seen quite a few in TV shows and films. They were all neat and clean, their walls adorned with paintings and designs. Thirty Thou Hong and I had sat with our backs to a wall, and when I'd turned to the side I could read, *Hey, Old H, give me back my money or I'll fuck your wife!* Then, in a different handwriting: *Feel free, I*

just married a Big White Pig from Changbai Mountain.
Above and to the side: *Brothers and sisters, come find me
if you want mutton soup, I'm at the little table.* All kinds
of messages, sketches of genitals smushed together, the
sort of thing you saw in public toilets. I hadn't liked
that wall covered in scribbled-over paper.

Back on the roof, I told Xingjian and Miluo about
Baolai's dream, and they burst out laughing.

"All right, Baolai," said Xingjian. "Now you're
ready to live life in the capital!"

Miluo said, "You've got two legs up on me. But
make sure we drink for free. Oh, and I'm going to draw
a whole row of big white asses on the wall."

"Don't forget the money! Just the old man's head,
10,000 each."

We picked up our game again, and surprise surprise, Baolai got the ace of spades every single round.
Afterward he had to pour us more beer and offer us
cigarettes, and while we smoked and drank, we chatted about Baolai's bar as if it was all a done deal. The
more we talked, the more we admired Baolai's vision
and how elegantly he'd set up the whole place. How
quickly we got used to spending that imaginary money.

Suddenly, Xingjian said, "Hey, Baolai, how come
you want to open a bar anyway?"

"I like being around lots of people. It's lively. Fun."

"That still doesn't mean you have to let people
draw on your walls," Miluo said.

"If you're waiting for someone and they don't
come, just leave your number. A sort of message board,
that's all. I think it'll be good."

So that was it. Beijing's too big, and it's far too easy to lose people—it's important to leave your number. He was actually onto something there. It didn't feel like an idea Baolai would have come up with on his own, unless we'd all underestimated him. Certainly it made the tone of our conversation more serious. Xingjian and Miluo were no longer talking about women and money. Holding the beers they'd won, they paced the roof, their gaze reaching into the distance. The sun had almost set, and light was draining from the sky. Far from us, the tall buildings darkened and then quickly lit up again. One by one, the lights of the city rippled on. As night arrived in Beijing and the city seemed even richer, the two of them grew anxious. They wanted something other than glimpsing women's thighs and the abstract notion of wealth. I completely understood. Deep down, they thought of a "career" as that "something else." Of course, *career* is a weighty word, and they were embarrassed to say it out loud. As far as I could tell, for all of Xingjian and Miluo's cunning plans, they had no idea what their futures might hold. All they had was a vague feeling of aspiration and the desire to "achieve something big." They'd only finished middle school and didn't know any more than I did. Even so, the idea of transforming their lives and "achieving something big" was serious. Just like they were now, hands on their hips, holding their beers, cigarettes drooping from their lips, looking melancholy.

"Fuck it, sooner or later I'm going to own a whole floor of that building, the one where the lights just came on," said Miluo. It was impossible to tell which distant skyscraper he was pointing at. He sounded like the Secretary General of the UN addressing the entire world.

"Even if it doesn't work out, it'll still be worth it if we get to die in this place." That was Xingjian. It seemed to me Xingjian wasn't quite as sharp as Miluo, and Miluo only conceded to him because he was bigger. Perhaps those broad shoulders provided cover.

It was completely dark now. The glow from the alley wasn't enough for us to make out the cards. Flocks of pigeons began coming home, a ring of coos all around us. The sluggish night air was suddenly made clear and deep by the pigeons' cries. We needed to grab some food and get ready for work.

*

I held the stamps made from yams and carrots, and Baolai carried the ink and sponge. Once again, we passed by Blossoms Bar. Only when I saw the fake barber pole did I realize I'd been seeing it every day for a month now. Our previous route had taken us past the donkey-burger shop and a lamb stew place, and when we were done eating, any bus from the stop just a few steps away would take us back into town. Baolai remained quiet, apparently deep in thought, and I decided not to question him about it out of respect.

A little before six o'clock, he once again climbed down from the roof to go buy beer. I volunteered to go with him to exercise my weak nerves. Out of necessity, I'd become addicted to running. Breathing hard, we reached Blossoms. Baolai slowed down as we passed, and his head swiveled until it had twisted almost all the way round as he peered inside. On our way back with the beer, he stared into the bar again, stopping once we got past it. Wiping his brow, he asked, "Did you see the person by the window? Did they have long or short hair?"

"Who?"

"Sitting by the plate glass window to the right of the door."

I had no memory of this, but then I hadn't really been looking.

"Help me see. Just check whether her hair's long or short."

I doubled back, and sure enough a girl was slumped over with her head on the table. I couldn't see her face, and it wasn't easy to tell the length of her hair. Amid the chaos of the bar, all I could hear was the loud thumping music and screeching voices. She was so still, I thought she might have fallen asleep. I picked up a pebble from the rubble around the utility pole and lobbed it at the glass, being careful not to use too much force. Her head moved a little. Long hair, or at least you wouldn't call it short. I went back and told Baolai. He said "oh," and his face drooped with disappointment.

"Were you looking for someone?" I asked.

"She has short hair."

"Who is she?"

"I don't know."

"If you don't know, why are you looking for her?"

Even with my weak nerves, I could see that Baolai

was in trouble—he'd fallen in love with a girl he didn't know. I tried to hold it back, but my laughter forced its way out. "Do you want to open your bar just to serve one person?"

"Don't make fun of me." Baolai's face was bright red. "And don't tell Xingjian and Miluo. Not one word."

"Tell me the truth, then."

Baolai blabbered a bit longer, insisting I had to keep it a secret. He wasn't sure of his own feelings; all he knew was the first time he saw her, he felt a soft bone somewhere in his body click, like a tiny dagger slotting into its sheath. "Have you ever seen someone just staring into space, and suddenly your heart hurts and you feel sad?" Baolai asked, coming to a halt again. I swung the beer bottles a little to indicate he should go on. One afternoon, about a month ago, he'd been making a phone call to my uncle from the newsstand diagonally across from the bar. Then he turned, and in the seat by the window was a short-haired girl. She was sitting very upright, her chin a little sharp, and she was staring into space. A bottle of beer sat on the table in front of her, and next to it was a red drink with a straw—possibly watermelon juice, possibly not. She was so still she could have been a statue, and her blank stare made it clear that she saw nothing. Just sitting there, like a daydreaming student in class. For no reason, Baolai decided she must be very sad, and her posture proved this. Her skin was pale and looked fragile. That's when Baolai heard that click deep in his body, the tiny dagger sliding home. A surge of pain through his heart. That was all: a little heartache, a scolding from my uncle for getting distracted and losing the thread of their conversation. Nothing more.

He saw her again the next day while making another phone call. It would have meant nothing, but the tiny dagger slipped farther into its sheath. The third time he saw her, he'd just been to the supermarket to buy us umbrellas because it was raining. I remembered that time—we'd been at home and wanted to go out for some food after we got tired of playing cards, but we had no umbrellas. We were always losing our umbrellas while out pasting ads. Xingjian and Miluo said to forget the cigarettes and beer; that day's penalty would be umbrellas. So Baolai set off to get them, and as he passed by the bar, he saw the girl sitting in the same place, this time in a golden yellow outfit. For some strange reason, he felt sad again. A gold dress against such delicate skin ought to have made him feel joyful and invigorated, yet on her it felt sorrowful somehow. Her back wasn't as straight as before. She was staring into space again but this time was twisted around to look out the window at the rain. Through the downpour and steamed glass, Baolai could see a slim, white cigarette between her index and middle fingers. She'd wiped the moisture from a patch of window, and Baolai was able to meet her eyes as he walked by. It felt the same as when he was pasting ads and caught sight of a police officer: His legs trembled and he almost fell into a puddle.

After that, Baolai began noticing that for whatever reason, at six o'clock each day, a dagger in his body needed a sheath, just like my panic attacks arrived punctually between four and five each day. He'd climb down from the roof and find some excuse to jog by to look, just to look. The girl was a regular. Every day around six, she'd be there sitting by the window, all alone, going through the same actions in turn: staring into space, smoking, sipping a beer or soft drink. Her posture would be either perfectly upright or a tiny bit slouched, though occasionally she'd slump right over onto the table and it would be hard to tell if she'd fallen asleep.

No wonder Baolai brought me out for a run whenever my head ached—it wasn't purely for my sake. Counting back using my fingers, I must have jogged by here with him at least ten times. Clearly I wasn't the brightest bulb.

"What happened next?"

"You know what. She hasn't been here for three days now."

"Do you think she knows who you are?"

"I don't know."

I laughed again. He'd be better off fantasizing about some twenty-eight-year-old woman like Xingjian. If I'd told the other two, they'd probably have thought he wasn't just an idiot, but a full-on lunatic. I'd heard of love at first sight, but never through a pane of glass. Oh my god, Baolai.

"I'm not going to do anything," said Baolai, his face tense. "I'm just worried about her."

Okay, then, if you have nothing better to do, feel free to worry about her. That's the closest you'll get to her, though. I did want to get a look at that girl myself. She must have been very gloomy and sad indeed for Baolai to get so hung up on her.

*

For the next ten days, driven by weak nerves and enormous curiosity, I went on long runs with Baolai that took us past Blossoms Bar. Jogging alleviated my headaches and tension but did nothing to alleviate my curiosity—the girl never showed. If a young woman happened to be in that seat, even if Baolai was certain it wasn't her, he still had me go check. He couldn't let it go. One day, when I'd gotten all sweaty from running and my brain felt exceptionally clear, I began to suspect that the woman Baolai was so concerned about might not exist at all.

"No, she really does exist. She was sitting right there." Baolai was very insistent, but the seat he was pointing at happened to be occupied by a long-haired guy. "Y…you don't b…believe me?"

Now he'd started stammering, I felt I had to keep going with him at least for a few more days. Anyway, whether or not she showed up, the jogging was good.

Another five days passed with no luck. I decided I would run only for the sake of my weak nerves—I shouldn't bother having any curiosity about this world. Baolai was losing weight from all the exercise, and his face looked somewhat deflated, which made him seem even more despairing with each passing day. Trying to comfort himself as much as me, he said no news was good news; no sign of her meant everything was fine. Out of habit, I argued back: "Why couldn't it be bad news?" He seemed confused for a moment, then grabbed his fleshy earlobes and tugged frantically at them. Those earlobes were the envy of my parents. My ma kept saying, "If only your earlobes were as big as Baolai's. Big earlobes mean good fortune. The Buddha's are so large they touch his shoulders." I wondered if Baolai's ears were like that because he was always tugging at them. If I did the same, mine would probably be elongated too. He spent ten minutes leaning against the utility pole and pulling his ears, then he gritted his teeth, stamped his feet, and said, "Bro, do me a favor. Go in and ask if anything happened to that girl."

Me? Just wandering in like a dumbass? Who would I even be asking about? People would think there was something wrong with me!

"Come on, brother, just this once. I'll buy your train ticket for when you go home for New Year, even if I have to get in line at midnight!"

That wasn't a bad offer. Buying a ticket from Beijing Train Station as New Year approached was as difficult as getting a postgraduate spot at Peking University... I'd heard that from a guy who'd wanted a fake Peking U degree cert. I pushed open the door and went up to the bar. The bartender asked what I wanted to drink, and I said I was looking for someone. Pointing at the seat by the window, I asked what happened to the short-haired girl who often sat there.

"Oh, her? No idea. She hasn't been here for a while. Are you her friend?"

"Mm, thanks anyway."

I went back outside. Baolai said, "Did you find out her name?"

"You didn't tell me to."

"Go ask. I'll treat you to KFC later."

I went back in. The bartender didn't know her name either. They didn't ask customers for their names. As I turned to leave, she suggested I check the wall-paper near that seat, to see if there were any clues. I went over, and between the beefy shoulder of a thirty-something bald man and the window, I saw a couple of lines in a slender, feminine scrawl: *If it's dark and you still don't want to go home, just let me know. The famous "Sitting Upright Girl."* Followed by a pager number. I asked the server if the girl was "Sitting Upright Girl," and she said maybe. I asked for pen and paper to take down the number.

Baolai stared at the paper and swore it had to be her. Because she always sat with her back straight, and didn't leave till almost dark? Either Baolai's intuition was superb, or he was confused. Either way, time for KFC.

*

Baolai carried Sitting Upright Girl's pager number around all day but never used it. He didn't dare. I tried several times to persuade him. "All you have to do is say it's dark but you don't want to go home either." He still didn't dare. He actually picked up the phone once but started trembling and hung up after only dialing a couple of digits. He'd begun sweating immediately. Another time, I offered to make the call myself, and though he eventually agreed after a lot of persuading, he grabbed the receiver and hung up before I could get through. It was torture for Baolai, not seeing her and being too scared to get in touch. We were still passing by the bar each day, but there was no sign of her. It was as if she'd evaporated into thin air.

If things went on like this, Baolai would get even crazier, or maybe snap altogether. I switched tactics and tried to shock him out of his obsession. For all we knew, she might be a Beijing girl, I told him, and what Beijinger would marry a penniless migrant worker like him? Let alone if she heard what he did for a living. Forget her. Baolai hung his head as if he'd been caught doing something wrong and said he didn't expect anything to happen; he was just worried—he sensed something was wrong. I said, "You don't know anything about her life. I sense something's wrong with *you*." He responded that I was young and didn't understand. Well, fine. I couldn't be bothered to understand that dogshit logic of his.

Life went on. We pasted up ads, played cards, and jogged. Like beetles, we circled round and round the bar. Another month passed. Baolai got even thinner, while my nerves slowly gained strength. As we ran past the bar one evening, he abruptly said, "I paged her."

I didn't understand.

"I called her pager."

I waited.

"It's a dead number."

I stopped running and leaned against the utility pole, breathing hard. This unexpected development caught me off guard. Even though we hadn't spoken about Sitting Upright Girl in a while, and even though it was Baolai who had the piece of paper with her number, I felt my pockets getting heavier. They seemed to weigh even more as we made another lap past the bar, until I thought my back would give out. Our lives were so monotonous. Apart from the cops, money, abstract ideas of struggle and ambition, and the steadily growing homesickness, Sitting Upright Girl was the most important thing in our lives, Baolai and me. I'd watched as anxiety, yearning, and vigorous exercise had transformed Baolai from a pudgy man to a trim figure. This kind man, who'd run the streets and alleys of Beijing with me, now had sadness written all over his face. I felt as if Sitting Upright Girl, who no longer existed, was clinging to him as tight as a shadow. Could someone I'd never seen, and whom Baolai had only glimpsed a few times through glass, be this important? It would seem so. Holding on to the utility pole to keep upright, I said, "Baolai…"

His lips parted a little. Why even bother smiling? "It's fine. Let's go another round. Is your headache better?"

I didn't mention it again. My nerves were still weak. Baolai was still a moron. We worked, slept, played cards, talked in theoretical terms about women and our dreams. We ran faster and faster.

One afternoon in late autumn, with a chill in the air and the city covered in fallen yellow leaves, we got out of bed and climbed up to the roof. Just as we'd started playing cards, my pager went off. It was Home. Ma paged every time she thought of me. I dropped my cards and went off to the newsstand across from Blossoms, where the public phone was. Halfway through talking with my mother, I suddenly hung up. A short-haired girl with a very straight back was sitting by the plate glass window, smoking. *That* seat. Her face was tilted out, and her eyes were as cloudy as the smoke coming from her lips. I was sure this was Sitting Upright Girl. Without even waiting for my change from the news-stand guy, I dashed back to the pingfang, shouting as I got close, "Baolai! Come down here! Quick!"

Baolai didn't dare believe I'd seen the right girl, but he ran back to the bar with me. As we got closer, I saw three men dressed head to toe in denim hauling her out of the bar. One of them had a shaved head, one a crew cut, and the third the sort of center-part that villains have in TV dramas. The girl was clearly unwill-ing—she was rearing back with all her strength and clinging to the door frame. Shaved Head wasn't very tall, but he was strong. He squeezed her wrist until the pain made her let go. By the time we got there, she was being dragged out, legs trailing on the ground, toes scrabbling to find purchase. Her legs left no mark on the damaged asphalt as she was pulled along.

She screamed, "I won't go! Let me go! Please, I'm begging you! I don't want to go!"

No one paid any attention. After the door of the bar closed behind her, nothing could be heard from inside, and no one came out. Baolai shouted, "Let go of her! Let go!" He wasn't as fast a runner, but he still managed to pass me. He grabbed Crew Cut's arm. "Let her go! You can't do that to a woman!" I caught hold of TV Villain's arm, but his elbow smashed into my chin, and I fell to the ground. Baolai managed to get Crew Cut to let go of the girl, but they outnumbered us. The girl was crouched down, sobbing in terror, too shocked to even run. By the time I'd gotten to my feet, Crew Cut and Shaved Head had flung Baolai to the ground.

"Run! Quick!" he shouted.

The girl didn't move, and neither did I. It was all too fast for me. I'd never been in a fight like this.

"Quick! Go!" Baolai shouted again. "Get Xingjian and Miluo!" His voice strangled at the end, because the two of them were kicking him in his back. I tried to go help him, but TV Villain tripped me and the next thing I knew, I'd cut my lip on the road.

"Run!"

I climbed to my feet and started sprinting. TV Villain couldn't catch up. I felt myself going faster and faster. The autumn wind swept under my arms like a pair of wings. I felt a sort of satisfaction as I ran, faster and faster, faster and faster, faster and faster, only my toes touching the ground, my body as light as if I were doing the tiny water steps from *Demi-Gods and Semi-Devils*. It may have been the fastest I ever ran in my life. Quick as I could, I called up to Xingjian and Miluo. They ran back with me, each holding a stool, cursing all the way. We might be broke, we might be struggling to survive, but we would not be bullied. Even though it felt as if we'd flown there, we were too late. We found Baolai alone, slumped against the utility pole. No sign of the girl or the three guys. He was bleeding from his forehead. They must have bashed his head against the pole. There was a bloodstain on an ad for treating stomach ulcers.

I cradled Baolai's head and called his name, weeping. Xingjian and Miluo were frustrated that they hadn't gotten to fight. They sat on either side of us, on their stools, just staring. I yelled, "Call an ambulance, you idiots!"

They stared at me, eyes wide. "An ambulance? How can we do that?"

"Dial 120!"

The street was empty. The door to the bar remained shut. I couldn't see how many people were inside, but not one of them came out.

Baolai's eyes drifted open and his lips moved. "Was it her?" he asked, then his eyes shut again.

That was the last coherent thing he said, and maybe would be for the rest of his life.

*

At the hospital, they said he had a severe concussion—something had come unstuck in his brain. Perhaps he could be cured, but it would cost a lot of money, a bottomless pit. Baolai's parents came to Beijing. They said even if they sold everything they had, including themselves, they still wouldn't be able to raise the sum the doctor had quoted. My uncle Thirty Thou Hong contributed ten thou, which was a huge sum at the time. He wept as he left the room, sadness digging at his heart. *Do you think it was easy for me to earn that money?* he said to anyone who would listen. *It's not like it was a workplace injury.* That 10,000 yuan was the most money Baolai's parents had ever seen in their lives. They had nothing to say about it. The three men were never caught, and we never found the girl. All in all, I gave four statements, and each time I told the cops every last detail I could remember. One young officer seemed very curious about the girl. He asked if I was sure she was the woman who called herself Sitting Upright Girl. I recalled the last thing Baolai said to me by the utility pole and ruefully shook my head. For many years after that, I would wish, even in my dreams, that I could have been sure it was her.

Without being able to track down the culprits, there was pretty much no way the crime would ever be solved. After a period of convalescence, Baolai returned to Huajie. He spent each day drifting in and out of consciousness. Even at his most lucid, he still needed to wear a towel around his neck, because his drooping mouth could not stop dribbling.

We were sad for a very long time about what happened to Baolai. One afternoon, when the trees had lost their leaves, there wasn't a whisper of wind, and the early winter sunlight felt infinite, Miluo got up and had a sudden impulse. Climbing up and down from the roof quite a few times, he swept it clean and moved the table and stools up there, all ready to play Ace of Spades with Xingjian and me. We all wanted to lighten the mood, but after a bit of chat, we just played in silence. Our hands full of cards, putting them down one at a time, no one knowing where the ace might be. It was impossible to guess with Baolai gone. Then all the cards were played, but we still hadn't seen it.

"That's impossible," Miluo mumbled. "I counted

the cards—they were all there. I definitely saw the ace of spades."

The three of us searched under the table, under our stools, in our pockets, all over the roof, everywhere. The ace of spades was nowhere to be found. Spooky. Xingjian and Miluo looked suspiciously at me. I spread my hands, and just like that my face was all wet. I felt as if I'd waited a long time for those tears to come.

IF A SNOW
STORM
STORM
STORM
STORM
STORM
STORM
STORM
STORM
STORM
STORM
STORM
STORM
STORM
STORM
SEALS
THE DOOR

If a Snowstorm Seals the Door

Winter was just arriving in Beijing when Baolai had his wits beaten out of him and went back to Huajie. Icy winds pawed at the doorframe and blew into the house. The PVC curtain had split down its length, becoming an icy whistle for the slightest gust of air. Xingjian, huddling beneath the covers, said, "Leave it alone; I don't believe a goddamn person could freeze to death in the capital." So, I put down the thumbtacks and plastic bags and crawled back into bed. The wind whistled softly in the house and loudly outside. From my nest of blankets, with my eyes shut, the northwest wind was a great black flood over the rooftops. Baolai's little wooden stool tumbled over and was dragged from one end of the roof to the other. Despite all that gusting wind I could hear the stool, clomping overhead like a fat man in size 41 hard-soled boots. The day Baolai was taken back to Huajie, I handed his Wanli leather shoes to his father, who held them up against his suitcase, then flung them into the trash can by the door: "They're full of holes anyway." His wooden stool had been abandoned too, left on the roof to be blown this way and that.

The next morning, I climbed up to retrieve the stool. The night's northerly wind had scoured the roof cleaner than water ever could. Several years' accumulation of dirt and debris was gone, revealing the tar-coated surface. The stool was wedged into the southeast corner and took some effort to dislodge. I blew invisible dust from its surface and sat down. The sky had been blown clean too, like a calm lake. My head abruptly started to hurt, and just then a flock of pigeons wheeled in from the south, the whistles attached to their tails like distant gongs. I yelled down from the rooftop, "They're here!"

The pair of them climbed up, rolling down their padded sleeves with slingshots in their mouths. There could be no greater pleasure this deep in the winter than a chicken in the pot, unless it was an even tastier pigeon. "They're good for you," said Miluo. "Good for both yin and yang. If a pregnant woman ate ninety-nine pigeons, she'd be sure to have a son. And if a guy did the same thing, he could burrow his way through a heap of women and still emerge ready to go." I had no idea where he got these theories. But in the past month, the two of them had shot down five birds.

I didn't hate pigeons, but their squawking got to me. An ancient, yellowing, gleaming sound, circling my head faster and faster, tighter and tighter, wrapping around my brain like the Monkey God's cursed metal band. My weak nerves were already a curse, another ring tightening around my mind. Because of their frequency and amplitude, the cries of pigeons were hard on my nerves, making my head throb so badly I felt like smashing it against a wall. If I were unlucky enough to be a pigeon and was forced to fly around with them, I'd surely have gone crazy.

"You'll never have to worry about being a pigeon," said Xingjian, "So just use your fingers to count out when they'll be flying by. Miluo and I will be in charge of taking them down."

There was no system; it was just by feeling. I'd read that bats could sense ultrasonic waves, and in the same way, pigeon noises chimed against my weak nerves from a distance. That morning the pigeons must have been touched in the head too—they made large loops over our roof, but out of slingshot range, leaving Xingjian and Miluo stomping their feet in frustration. They were barefoot in long underwear, their lips blue with cold. After expending all their stones, they grumbled all the way down from the roof, cursing those bastard pigeons. It was pointless. It's not like they followed any plan; they just flew where they wanted. In my long experience of weak nerves, at moments like that, the best way (apart from meds) to get rid of a headache was a jog. So I went for a run. The Beijing air was rarely that clear—a shame to waste it.

From the ground, I realized my position in relation to the pigeons had changed. Instead of circling around our roof, they were following the neighboring streets. Fuck it, I'd get rid of the lot of them. It must have been a fairly odd sight: a guy jogging through the alleyways of Beijing's western outskirts, his breath coming in white clouds, screaming at the sky as he ran, a flock of pigeons above him. After fifteen minutes or so, I hadn't scared away a single bird. They soared and plunged, all within that gigantic circuit. They weren't afraid of me. The more I gesticulated and waved at them, the higher and faster they flew. An observer might have thought they were fleeing from me. Then another morning jogger appeared behind me.

The pale, scrawny guy looked like he was in middle school; he was definitely younger than me. He kept his head down, hair poking up as if he were the kid brother of Lei Zhenzi, the thunder god in those cartoons. He kept my pace, speeding up or slowing down when I did, so we stayed a constant eight meters apart. His route was exactly the same as mine. A passer-by might have thought we were chasing pigeons together. On a track, there could be fifty people around you and it wouldn't be an issue, but in this chilly alleyway, one guy tailing me felt more uncomfortable than being stuck in a big crowd. It was a strange feeling, like being stalked, or copied, or threatened, even mocked—I felt somehow unclean. I didn't like it, anyhow. Something in his labored breathing made me feel this guy wouldn't be easy to deal with, but there was no need to bother. His scrawny frame could maybe manage to run 2,000 meters, but any more would surely wipe him out. No matter how determined he was to shadow me, I could easily shake him off. Instead, I stopped—a short run had been enough to make my head feel right. It would soon start aching anew, though, so even I had no idea when I might need to suddenly dash off again.

The next day, when I came down from the roof, pigeons flew in from the south once more, so I had to shoo them off before they could settle. Xingjian and Miluo, complaining of the cold, had refused to leave the warmth of their beds. I ran toward the birds, howling. They soared away, but then I sensed another person's footsteps on my scalp. When your nerves are weak and you have a headache, every little movement feels like it's happening directly on your skull. I turned to see the kid from the day before. He was in a ski jacket, his hair waving in the breeze as softly as Chang Yu-sheng's. I chased the pigeons south of Seventh Alley before stopping and watching as he ran past me. He followed the pigeons.

*

Xingjian and Miluo shot down two more birds. They tumbled from the sky like broken tridents, knocking their beaks crooked on the icy cement path. Stewed pigeon is truly delicious, and in the deep winter air, clear as glass, the aroma travels more than fifty meters. Nibbling on a slim pigeon neck and sipping broth, I came to the conclusion that it was at least twice as good as chicken soup. In the cold weather, the pigeons had grown fatty and meaty.

If I were those pigeons, after the loss of so many comrades, I certainly wouldn't go anywhere near our rooftop. But the pigeons weren't me, and they continued to fly past once or twice a day. Chasing pigeons became a form of exercise—I ran and ran, which was good for my weak nerves. I had nothing to do during the day, anyway. The third time I saw the young man, he wasn't behind me, but right before my eyes. I turned down the alleyway where the donkey-burger place was, and the kid, clenching his fists, came right up to me.

"Have you seen my pigeons?" He spoke Mandarin with a southern accent. You could tell he wished he looked fiercer.

Oh. "Your pigeons?" I gestured overhead. The birds were killing me with their racket.

"I've lost two more of them!"

"If my head keeps aching from their racket, I'll chase them all to Vietnam."

"I've lost two more pigeons."

"So, you've been following me?"

"I saw you." His gaze suddenly turned awkward. "At the entrance of Blossoms Bar. I saw the fat guy getting beaten up.

"I couldn't help you," he added. "My bicycle's kickstand was broken, and the basket was full of pigeons. I could only shout for help. I called out: 'There's a fight, someone's getting killed, come quick!'"

I had absolutely no recollection of hearing that southern-accented Mandarin. But I did recall the stench of fresh chicken shit, only it must have been pigeon. He couldn't have helped us anyway, shrimp that he was.

"You raise pigeons?"

"I herd them," he said. "But if you haven't seen my pigeons, I'll be off."

It was just as well that he left, since I didn't know how to explain the seven birds he was missing. I thought back to the three of us eating and drinking, belching with satisfaction. Seven was not a small number.

After that, when I saw the pigeons flying overhead, I no longer called out to wake Xingjian and Miluo. When I chased them as I jogged, there was no longer a shadow behind me. I knew I'd betrayed his trust, but had no idea if he knew that too. Feeling guilty, I didn't mind as much the pigeons cooing. Walking down the main road, I felt an affinity for anything that could fly. Even a plastic bag caught on the telephone wire would transfix me for a while.

One day at noon, I had to go to Thirty Thou Hong's for some ink. Passing along Zhongguancun High Street, I saw a flock of pigeons scuttling back and forth on the pavement outside Modern Plaza. They looked familiar. Even though it was freezing cold, young parents had brought their children to play with the birds, and couples flashed ruddy cheeks as they took selfies. I knew how it worked—you bought a bag of pigeon feed and got to pose for photographs with them. Then I spotted a loner sitting among the flock of birds and humans, his head so low that practically his whole neck had retreated inside his coat collar. It was an exceptionally cold winter, and even the sunlight seemed sickly. His hair was soft, his head small, and his face pale. Clear snot dripped from his nose. I walked up to him and said, "One bag of feed."

"It's you!" He stood, four little sacks of pigeon food falling from their hooks on his coat.

They were tiny plastic bags that held maybe eighty to a hundred grains of wheat, one-fifty each. I helped pick them up. Nearby were two pigeon cages and an old Flying Pigeon brand bicycle, covered in bird shit, leaning against a lattice fence. As he'd said, the kickstand was broken. This was his flock—plaza pigeons. I got to feed each of them two kernels of food for free. He gave me his folding stool, spreading newspaper over the welded steel bars of the cage as a seat for himself.

"There are fewer and fewer pigeons," he said, pulling his neck down into his coat collar.

"You cold?"

"Even the pigeons are cold."

*

The southerner was named Lin Huicong, and he turned out to be two years older than me. His home was so far away it was practically the southernmost point of China. At the end of last year, he'd finished his exams, but his essay wasn't good, so he didn't even get into one of the vocational schools. Of course, where he came from, a spot in a vocational school was considered a good result. The exam consisted of a passage that he had to respond to, followed by an open-ended essay topic. The passage was this: Three trees per person per year, a hillside requires a 100,000 trees, each spring day requires 1.3 billion trees, and so forth. Quite poetic. The essay topic was "If..." Throwing caution to the wind, he wrote on "If a Snowstorm Seals the Door." To be honest, many of the exam graders down south wouldn't even have seen snow in their whole lives and certainly couldn't imagine enough of it that it would seal a door shut. He wrote voluminously about planting trees and snowstorms, all muddled together with no apparent logic. The examiner thought he'd gone so far off the rails, he didn't score even half of the 150 points allowed.

His father asked him, "What do you have to say for yourself?"

His reply was, "I'm going to Beijing."

In China, if you ask any given person where they're going, the majority will tell you Beijing. Lin Huicong was heading there too, but not to see Tiananmen Square. He wanted to know what snow looked like. Also, he had an uncle who lived there. Many years ago, this uncle stabbed someone and, thinking the victim was dead, hopped the Beijing train that very night. He'd been a poultry yard worker and had pulled out his knife after losing his temper over a cockfight. He never came back but would occasionally send money home, giving the impression he'd made it big. Lin Huicong's ba pridefully declared, "That's fine, go and stay with your uncle; you can live the good life in Beijing too." So Huicong bought a standing-room-only train ticket to the capital. When he took off his shoes after the journey, his feet had swollen into two huge, misshapen loaves.

His uncle didn't, as he'd imagined, greet him in an impeccable suit. In fact, his clothes—speckled with dubious gray-white spots like stars—were even sloppier than what folks wore back home. Nose streaming, Lin Huicong asked, "Still covered in chicken shit?"

"No, pigeon!" the uncle said and spat onto his fingers to carefully rub a speck of the stuff from his granddad shirt. "This stuff is clean!"

After taking on quite a few odd jobs in Beijing,

Huicong's uncle had decided that his old line of work was more reliable after all, only he'd raise pigeons instead of chickens. Who knows how he'd been so goddamn lucky as to get this job tending plaza pigeons. He was in charge of taking care of them, transporting them to various public spots and landmarks at particular times for the pleasure of both residents and tourists. It might not seem like a particularly impressive position, but it paid quite well and—being a public service—was funded from above. In addition, you got to sell feed at one-fifty per bag and keep all the proceeds, no matter how many you sold. There had been getting to be more pigeons than he could manage, so his nephew arrived at just the right time. He handed over two cages of birds and charged him nothing but a commission of fifty cents per bag of feed. He told Huicong he could easily provide for himself with his share.

"How's that going?" I asked, knowing that most solitary people in Beijing aren't particularly able to fend for themselves.

"I manage," he said. "Only, it's a little cold."

The winter sun set early, and as soon as the light began to fade, everyone raced off home. It was indeed cold, and there were fewer and fewer people, making the pigeons seem more numerous. Huicong decided to close up shop for the day. He blew a peculiar whistle and the birds waddled over to the cage, their shoulders hunched too.

Huicong lived on South Seventh Alley. I wouldn't have called living there "managing"—the heat didn't work. It was a pretty basic place. His landlady was a stingy old woman who kept a coal stove in her own room, practically wrapping herself around it all day long. As long as she was warm, she didn't care about her tenant, only tossing a piece of coal into the boiler when she thought of it, and if she forgot, so be it. Often, Huicong would brush against the radiator during the night, only to be shocked awake by its icy coldness. When he complained, the old lady said, "Well, I haven't charged you a single cent extra for your pigeons!" Huicong responded, "The pigeons don't live in the house." "The courtyard is mine too," she retorted, "and if we went by headcount, you'd owe me more than 10,000 a month." Huicong shut up at once. His flock—even if each bird cooed just a couple of times—collectively sounded like an unbearably noisy gaggle whispering to each other all night long. He was lucky the old woman hadn't fought him about that.

"I'm scared of the cold." Huicong said, sounding ashamed of being a frost-fearing southerner. "But I have been hoping to see a proper snowstorm."

The storm would come. The weather report had said a cold front from Siberia was approaching the city, although forecasts weren't always accurate, and half the time you didn't know what on earth they were talking about. But still I told him that the storm would definitely arrive. If it didn't snow, what kind of winter would that be?

Purely out of pity, when I got home I told Xingjian and Miluo about Huicong and asked them how they'd feel about him coming to live with us. Our heating was good—the landlord, a bicycle repairman, liked strong spirits, so every few days we'd send him a small bottle of sorghum liquor. He quickly started treating us like family, and the heat blazed unsparingly. At times, when we were too lazy to go out for food, he'd even let us use his charcoal stove. That's how we'd roasted the seven pigeons.

"Sure," said Miluo, "but what if he finds out we ate seven of his birds?"

"So what!" snapped Xingjian. "Let him move in; his rent money will buy us beer. And he'll have to bring us a gift, won't he? A couple of pigeons or something."

I skipped off to South Seventh Alley. Huicong very much wanted to come live with us, but he wouldn't give up any of his pigeons—he said he'd happily buy us an old mother hen instead. I helped Huicong move his stuff to our house, where he took Baolai's old bed. Along with his luggage, he brought the plucked chicken. At noon, Xingjian and Miluo were huddled around the stove, drooling as they watched the chicken soup simmer. Huicong and I were outside, building a new coop for the pigeons. It was very simple: a row of wooden boxes filled with dried grass and cotton wool. When the door was open, they'd go in, and when it was shut, they'd fall soundly asleep. Like us, the birds lived in communal quarters, three or four per box. We insulated it against the cold and wind with asbestos tiles, torn cardboard cartons, and cloth scraps. Exposed to the elements, it would have been a refrigerator.

That chicken was delicious, especially with the two bottles of sorghum liquor I'd gotten from the convenience store. After all that soup, I felt a bit dizzy, Xingjian and Miluo were parched, and Huicong was overheated. I needed to sleep, Xingjian and Miluo wanted to go out to find some women, and Huicong felt like getting some air on the roof. He'd often seen us up there playing cards. The wind had blown open the sky over the house. In the distance, smoke from the chimneys was getting swept apart by the wind. Xingjian and Miluo waved goodbye as they slunk out, ready to spend what little money they'd saved on someone pale and plump.

"I've always wanted to come up here," said Huicong, standing on Baolai's stool for extra height, gazing into the distance all around. "You put down a card, then look up and there's all of Beijing."

I told him there was nothing much to see, just skyscrapers and tower blocks, fuck all to do with us. Walking amid that forest of buildings, I always felt like I was in the canal back home, head underwater, plunged straight to the bottom, unsteadily splashing my way forward.

"I want to see a blanket of snow cover this city. Can you imagine how magnificent that'd be?" Huicong made a sweeping gesture that encompassed all of time and space.

He was back to his idea of a snowstorm big enough to seal the door. This ignited my imagination. If a blizzard wrapped itself around Beijing, what would I see from here on the roof? How clean might that pure white world look, pale silver with no beginning or end, the difference between rich and poor erased: leveling skyscrapers, raising humble dwellings, high and low being nothing more than differing amounts of snow. Beijing would be like the fairy tales I'd once read: untainted, peaceful, replete, harmonious. The people walking along in their thick coats would all be part of the same family.

"What would you do if a storm came?" Huicong asked.

I didn't know. I'd seen snow, and I'd seen snow-storms. On days of heavy snowfall in the past, I'd always been listless, not knowing what to do.

"I'd stomp my way through the thick snowdrifts, crunching across the whole of Beijing."

A few pigeons flew up from the courtyard, and the rest followed, an avalanche of flapping. Noise like ultrasonic waves. "Could you take those whistles off them?" I said, clutching my head.

"I'll do it now." Huicong started climbing down from the roof. "They're only there so the chicks can find their way home."

*

Training the pigeons to get used to their new home took Huicong quite a few days. He did it all with his off-pitch whistle. Now that they no longer had those little panpipes attached to them, I began to like the birds, watching them soar and dip each day, as if I'd found a new group of friends. But every couple of days, a few more of them would vanish. I couldn't work out why—there were no other flocks nearby, so it wasn't like they'd been stolen. It wasn't Xingjian or Miluo—I knew where they kept their slingshots. Or was it? We worked for different bosses on different schedules, and I had no way of knowing what they did behind my back. Besides, they seemed to have gotten even tighter ever since they'd slunk out together in search of women, and they stuck up for each other all the time. Huicong said he understood: Men who've fought, studied, or whored together always end up close friends. Fine, let's assume they were the pigeon pilferers. Where were they cooking their purloined birds?

Huicong didn't want to fling around accusations without proof. Living under the same roof, it might have led to tension. Anyway, Xingjian and Miluo swore with the utmost sincerity that they'd not killed any pigeons after those first seven.

Huicong and I went back to running after the pigeons. It was good exercise, and we could protect the little creatures at the same time. A couple of eco-warriors. We ran through pretty much every street and alley in the western outskirts. But the birds kept vanishing, and the snow refused to fall. Each day he let them loose in some square or scenic spot, and at night I pasted ads in the streets and residential estates. Each time we left or came home we'd do a headcount, and if the number was right we'd be overjoyed, as if we'd avoided a robbery; if one had gone missing, we'd sink into unhappy silence, mourning the lost bird. After a while of this, Huicong said out of the blue, "It's because pigeons are so damn nutritious. When I started in the business, my uncle warned me that people always have their eye out for our birds."

But there was nothing we could do, even knowing this. There are only so many precautions you can take. It's not like you can bring pigeons to bed with you.

On the night the Siberian cold front came, it was incredibly windy. Xingjian, Miluo, and I were stuck indoors, unable to work, so we decided to have a little party, using rock-paper-scissors to decide which of us would be in charge of getting the booze, snacks, and donkey burgers. We stewed a pot of cabbage and beef, all four of us huddled around the stove and drinking till one in the morning, trying to work out from the whistling wind through the door just how cold it had gotten outside. Beijing went through a night of gusts and rumbling, interspersed with the sounds of countless objects colliding. We got quite drunk and felt as if the world had fallen into chaos.

The next day, Huicong got up first. He stepped outside and quickly came back in, standing at the foot of our beds holding four stiff pigeons, his little face ready to burst into tears. The birds had been lying frozen in front of their coop. He had no idea how they could have gotten out, nor how the wooden door had slammed shut behind them. Before we'd started drinking, we'd checked every one of those boxes, making sure that even if they'd been transported to Siberia itself, the pigeons would remain warm and alive inside. But here they were, incontrovertibly icy and dead. They must have pecked at the door for a long time before finally burrowing their beaks into the soft down under their wings and waiting for death.

"Did you hear those two get up during the night?" I asked Huicong.

"I drank too much. I slept like a corpse."

Me too. But I could guarantee Xingjian and Miluo had also been dead to the world—they couldn't hold their liquor at all. We could only say those four pigeons had been fated to die young. It would have been a shame to throw them away, so Miluo offered to cook them. I hastily waved that suggestion away—I'd known those birds personally, and if they'd had names, I'd have used them. How could I eat them? That went double for Huicong. He handed the bodies over to Xingjian and Miluo, saying, "It's up to you, but don't let me see it." Then he walked out into the courtyard and squatted in front of the coop, staring intently at it, then up at the sky.

By the time we'd procrastinated our way through breakfast, it was after ten-thirty. Huicong carried his two cages of pigeons off to Xizhimen. Xingjian and Miluo glanced sidelong at each other, stuffed the dead birds into a plastic bag, and went out. I followed them at a distance. I'd thought I'd walked down almost every street in the huge western outskirts, but after tailing those two, I realized I'd only ever seen a tiny fraction of the whole. Beijing is vast, and its outskirts are just as enormous.

After many winding turns, Xingjian knocked on a little door in an alley I didn't know. It was the side entrance to a dilapidated residential courtyard. A young woman leaned halfway out, her hair messy, curls obscuring her pale face. Her bright red jumper hugged her body and pushed her breasts firmly out. She took the plastic bag and set it on the ground, then wrapped her left arm around Xingjian and her right one around Miluo, pulling them to her chest, and after holding them there a moment, she patted their faces. Then she rubbed her arms a couple of times from the cold and shut the door. I hid behind the public bathroom, waiting for Xingjian and Miluo to pass by before I stepped out. They were debating something and high-fived each other when they were done.

All I'd remember later of the place they dropped off the pigeons was high walls, a narrow door, a glimpse of roof with black tiles, and a couple of clumps of shriveled grass huddled and swaying in the wind. No sounds apart from the natural world. That's all.

*

No one was sure how the pigeon population kept dwindling. We counted them first thing in the morning and last thing at night, but in between they went missing. I couldn't prove that Xingjian and Miluo were doing anything underhanded; the disappearances seemed to have nothing to do with them. They even made sure to leave their slingshots out where we could all keep an eye on them. Back when Baolai lived here, they'd never liked to hang out with the two of us, and now it was the same with me and Huicong. They'd go out together, talking about lofty topics like their ideals, making a fortune, women. From my rooftop perch, I'd occasionally see them wandering from one alley to another, winding their way to some far-off place. Of course, I couldn't tell if they'd gone knocking at that little door again. You can't make wild guesses about what you can't see.

There was nothing Huicong could do about the vanishing birds. "If only I could stuff them in my pockets," he lamented as we sat on the roof. "Then I'd know they were still there, wherever I went." Because of the poachers, it was inevitable that their numbers would keep dwindling, which filled him with anxiety. If his uncle were to find out what was going on, he'd put on a stern, businesslike face and warn his nephew that if he quit, he'd need to give back roughly the same number of birds as he'd been given. How roughly? Huicong felt the current flock was approaching that danger point. "I don't ask for much," he said, "I just want to see one snowstorm before I go." The sky above our heads was blue, the clouds white. The Siberian cold front had blown away all the dirt, and new pollution hadn't yet filled the air.

Why wouldn't the weather forecast predict another blizzard? They'd gotten it wrong the first time around, but just a few more predictions ought to fix that.

Pigeons kept going missing, and the snow stayed away. It was rare in the history of Beijing—a winter without proper snow. Huicong had practically given up on eating and sleeping to keep watch over his birds. When he let them loose during the day, he often asked me to keep him company on a run until they came home again. He usually woke up twice during the night, once at one-thirty and once at five, to head outside and make sure his flock was secure. Despite all his efforts, they continued going astray, and the tipping point drew closer. Even Xingjian and Miluo couldn't bear to watch, avoiding him when they got up in the night to pee. They urged Huicong to cheer up: "It's only a few pigeons; let your uncle take the rest back, and if all else fails, you can come work with us. They'll bury you when you're dead no matter where you are, and as long as you stay in Beijing, opportunity will find its way to you sooner or later."

Huicong protested, "You're not me, and I'm not you. I'm from the deep south."

One morning in January, I got back to the house after a jog and Xingjian yelled at me, his headphones still plugged into the radio, "Tell Huicong if he wants a snowstorm, he'll get one this evening."

"For real? That's the forecast?"

"The National Weather Bureau, the Beijing Weather Bureau, plus a bunch of random meteorologists all said so."

I stepped back outside and felt the sky instantly darken: lead-gray clouds fermenting above. Everything felt as if a blizzard was on its way. I found Huicong at the entrance to Modern Plaza. His uncle was there too, a beer-bellied guy with some kind of animal fur on his coat collar. "If you can't hack it, go home!" The uncle's hands were stuffed into his coat pockets, and he sounded like a village cadre. "Life in the capital isn't like back home; it's all about survival of the fittest." Huicong lowered his head. He hadn't had time to comb his hair that morning, and it stood up in clumps like Lei Zhenzi's once again. He was close to tears.

"All the experts say a snowstorm is on its way," I called as I drew up to them. "It's a sure thing. Two bags of birdfeed, please."

Huicong looked up, then at his uncle. "Just give me two more days. That's all."

*

On the way home, I bought some sorghum liquor and duck necks to snack on as we watched the snow fall over Beijing. Huicong ran outside five times before midnight, but there wasn't a single flake. The night sky was desolate and full of sadness. Then we fell asleep, and it was past ten the next morning when we were awakened by something scrabbling at the door. I tried to push it open, but it wouldn't budge. I pushed harder. Nothing. Then I had a burst of energy, and the earth and sky were white, the snow in front of the door up to my knees. I yelled at the others, "Quick, come see—the snowstorm sealed the door!"

Huicong darted out from beneath the covers in just his shorts and ran into the snowdrifts barefoot, shrieking senselessly in his southern dialect. Birds flapped above the courtyard and rooftops. On a day like this, sparrows and pigeons ought to stay in their nests instead of venturing out. Yet the flock of pigeons refused to stay still for a second, landing and pecking at the ground wherever they could, which was what had caused the scratching noise that woke us.

Two pigeons stood by the coop with their heads tilted. Snow had covered the wooden boxes. They were both dead but didn't look frozen or starved or suffocated. Xingjian said if he could take them, he'd supply our dinner and drinks that night—we ought to celebrate Beijing's biggest snowfall in thirty years. That's what the radio said—the drifts and flurries of the night were a three-decade record.

After a quick meal, Huicong and I climbed up

onto the roof. Post-blizzard Beijing wasn't quite the way I'd imagined. The snow didn't actually cover everything, and the glassy skyscrapers still twinkled murkily. Still, Huicong was very satisfied. He felt like Beijing was more solemn when blanketed in white, a sort of monochrome seriousness, the dark buildings like rocks by the shoreline protruding from the white foam of ocean waves. He made a snowball and nibbled at it, muttering as he gnawed, "This is snow. This is snow."

Xingjian and Miluo emerged, and we watched as they turned this way and that, meandering through the snow into the distance. Pigeons flew in circles over our heads. I counted them for Huicong—still just enough that he could hand them over to his uncle, but any fewer would be unacceptable. We walked back and forth on the roof, the new snow springy and loose beneath our feet. I told Huicong how Baolai used to say he wanted to play cards on the roof as snow covered the ground. But he hadn't been able to wait that long, and who knew if he'd ever play cards again.

I'm not sure how long we stayed on the roof—at least until our bellies started rumbling. That's when Xingjian and Miluo reappeared. We came down from the roof and saw Xingjian still holding the plastic bag with the dead pigeons.

"Fuck it, she's gone back home." He said, giving the wall a sharp kick and rattling the plastic bag. "Damn it all, she's gone back to her hometown to wait for death."

Miluo prized the bag from his hand and lit a cigarette. He said, "I'll find a place to bury these birds."

BROTHER

Brother

A young man in search of his twin passed between two enemy encampments. In those moments before the clamor of war erupted, he glanced left and right at the ranks arrayed on either side. The moonlight was bright, and as he turned to our side, where I stood hidden within the crowd, I saw him smile as if in a dream.

A week earlier he'd arrived in Beijing from a city in the south. He got off the train, shouldered his pack, and wandered the streets until he finally ended up living in the courtyard next to ours with a group of pirated DVD sellers from Jiangxi. He'd originally wanted to stay with us, but Xingjian and Miluo had turned him down, saying they were expecting family to visit. Of course, there was no family; they just thought he looked suspicious. After just a quick chat they sent him packing.

"Did you see the way he looked?" asked Xingjian, half-closing his eyes. "Sort of shifty, right?" I nodded. "A little wild, huh?" said Miluo. I nodded again. I had to admit Xingjian did a good impression: With his big eyes narrowed, he looked a million miles away.

They were certain something was wrong with the guy. And no wonder: What sane person would say he'd come to Beijing looking for his alter ego? He'd said to us, "There's another Dai Shanchuan in the world, right here in Beijing." "No kidding," we said. "You're bound to find a few people sharing any halfway normal name in a city of 20 million." But Dai Shanchuan corrected us, "No, not just the same name, the same person." The three of us instantly got goose pimples. The same person! Dai Shanchuan narrowed his eyes, looking past us with a distant gaze, like a crow gliding on wings above the city, flying from here in the western outskirts to Chaoyang District and onward to Tongzhou. We were sitting on the roof—the best hospitality we could offer—and had been hoping he would take the spot that had been Baolai's, then Huicong's, so we could split the rent four ways instead of three.

"Look: This is Beijing," said Xingjian, gesturing grandly from the roof at the sprawling city. "You won't find a better spot to live in this neighborhood. From this roof you can see the whole capital."

Dai Shanchuan nodded very slowly. "Yes, I'm sure I'll be able to find Dai Shanchuan from here."

"Are you sure it's really Dai Shanchuan you're looking for?" I asked.

"Not Lai Shenchan?" asked Xingjian.

"Or Kai Shanchang?" said Miluo.

"No," replied Dai Shanchuan, his smile quietly confident. Later, we all agreed that, no matter how you looked at it, there had been something off about that smile. "It's my other self I'm looking for."

Then he sat down in the one bamboo chair we

had up there and told us all about the Dai Shanchuan he was looking for, whose photo he'd grown up seeing. He pulled a crumpled three-by-five-inch snapshot from his wallet, showing a pale, pudgy baby, perhaps not even a year old, with a foolish grin and wispy brown hair. "Dai Shanchuan," he said. Then from another pocket he drew a second photograph, a boy of ten or so in a checkered suit, hands on hips and with that same foolish grin, hair hastily parted for the photo. "Me."

"You're Dai Shanchuan," said Xingjian.

"He is him; I am me."

"Dai Shanchuan is you," said Miluo.

"I am another him. He is another me."

What a mess.

Xingjian was the first to really suspect something was wrong. He pointed out a flock of pigeons flying overhead. "We should bring one of those little fuckers down for dinner."

Miluo and I both looked up at the passing flock. But Dai Shanchuan's gaze, still like a vast, gliding crow, saw no pigeons. He insisted on continuing the story about Dai Shanchuan.

In fact, the whole thing was very straightforward and might have happened to any of us. If you're naughty as a child, your father might say, "We should have kept the other one, not you." You have to admit it was a good trick: His little heart could barely stand the thought that some other kid might show up one day and put on his clothes, eat from his cup and bowl, and steal his parents' love, replacing him entirely. And so, he behaved—at least in that moment. That kind of half-serious deception usually only works for a few years. After you've grown up a bit, you stop falling for it. The adults lose interest in the gambit and go back to the tried-and-true beatings and scoldings. But Dai Shanchuan was different. He was an only child—the sole recipient of the affection of his grandfathers, grandmothers, aunts, uncles, cousins, and parents, who couldn't bear to be rough with him. Even his imaginary rival couldn't be someone else—the only possible rival he might have was himself. Even before he was a year old, if he refused his dinner, his grandparents would point at a photo in an elegant frame (the same one he'd pulled out of his pocket) and say, "Do you know who that is?"

Dai Shanchuan pointed at himself.

His grandparents shook their heads. "That's the you in Beijing."

Dai Shanchuan tottered over to the dressing table mirror, trying to reach in and fish himself out.

When he refused to nap, his grandparents would point at the photograph. "If you don't sleep, we'll trade you for that Dai Shanchuan."

Dai Shanchuan would hurriedly shut his eyes tight.

All any family member had to do was point toward that photograph, and Dai Shanchuan would behave. For years the person he feared most was not his mother or father, not his teacher, not the bad kids in class who smoked and brawled, not Ah Fei the local street tough, but that other self in that photograph. It was a fear verging on hatred. That self, way off in Beijing, was his greatest enemy. The photograph felt three-dimensional, and no matter what angle you viewed it from, the eyes seemed to follow you. When he was young, Dai Shanchuan would peek at the photo from the corner of his eye, but the self in Beijing always noticed, and it turned the poor boy into the most obedient child in the neighborhood. When he started school, he was a model student, and the teacher would encourage the other children to be like him. He thought of destroying the photograph but didn't dare to launch an open assault; instead, he pretended he'd broken the glass in a moment of accidental clumsiness. His parents didn't scold him; they simply had the photo remounted in an even more beautiful frame and hung it back where it had been. His father said, "You be careful with this now."

As he grew older, the Dai Shanchuan in the photo remained a year-old baby. Yet he found himself unable to leave himself behind. All those years, he'd had only himself as a friend. No brothers or sisters, and when he came home from school there was no one his age to play with. His family worried about his safety away from home, worried about the influence of wild children on his studies, worried he would trip and fall while running, worried he would get into fights. He could only play with the self on the wall, to whom he would say, "Hello, Dai Shanchuan."

Then he'd answer on his own behalf: "Hello to you, Dai Shanchuan."

"Have you eaten yet, Dai Shanchuan?"

"I have, Dai Shanchuan. Have you?"

"I have. Do you know the poem 'Climbing Stork Tower'?"

"Yes, I have it memorized: 'The sun beyond the mountains glows; The Yellow River seawards flows. You can enjoy a grander sight, by climbing to a greater height.'"

"Ma and Ba were fighting this morning. Do you know why?"

"Probably just the hot weather."

"They fight at night, too."

"Because the air conditioner is still broken."

"Today the teacher scolded me for not joining in with the other kids."

"That's because you've got me for a friend."

"Right, that's why."

Sure enough, photo-Dai Shanchuan became Dai Shanchuan's best friend. He liked talking to him and got used to the idea that he had this other self, also called Dai Shanchuan, living in an unfamiliar but very famous city. He was his own best friend, his only friend. When he was home alone, he was never lonely, because once he'd learned to be friends with himself, he never felt loneliness.

"Maybe you actually do have a twin brother?" I asked him.

"If you do," added Xingjian, "this whole thing would make a lot more sense. But having 'another self'...ha, that just sounds freaky."

"Unless maybe you have multiple personality disorder," said Miluo.

"All that occurred to me," said Dai Shanchuan, turning the photograph over and over. "But my parents said they'd only had one child. Could it really be possible for someone to have a doppelgänger?"

He pulled yet another photo from his pocket, this one obviously more recent. "Have you met anyone in Beijing who looks like this?"

Xingjian shivered a bit and grimaced. "I can't hold it any longer, I'm heading down for a piss."

As he started down Miluo followed him, and I stood up as well. Beijing was a big place, all kinds of weird stuff could happen, but this was just a bit too strange.

"But I'm not done with the story," said Dai Shanchuan.

"No need," said Xingjing, already down in the courtyard. "The bed won't be available for a bit; we've got some family visiting for a while. Right, guys?"

Miluo and I chimed in: "Yup, that's right."

And that was the end of that. As I saw Dai Shanchuan out, I motioned with my head toward the courtyard next door. "They ought to have a bed free; why don't you try there?"

The next morning, I had one of my pounding headaches and went for a run through the alleys. As I passed the open gate of the courtyard next door, someone called out to me in a muffled voice. I stuck my head in and saw Dai Shanchuan squatting at the water faucet, brushing his teeth. He waved to me, mouth full of foam.

*

We had no work at that time—it was impossible to paste ads. It was what they called "urban psoriasis": we were the itch and the cops were out to scratch us; even the street sweepers dropped their brooms and gave chase. All the vendors who wandered the streets—fruit sellers with their flatbed bikes, roadside DVD sellers, fake-ID merchants, buskers, hawkers of crepes or nuts or sausages or fruitcake or soy milk or buns or boxed lunches, peddlers of whistles or erhu or gourd-flutes— all of us hunkered down in our rented rooms. No one forbade us from going out, of course. But we'd be crazy to try. All of Beijing was being "cleaned up." The word was that a major political conference was coming up.

When everyone was busy making money, we got along okay—too busy to pursue grudges or rivalries. Now, with nothing else to do, it was time to settle scores, time to take up arguments, time to pick fights— anything to fill the hours. To start, the conflicts were specific. Mostly one on one and resolved with words as often as fists. But eventually things got messy: more fists and more fighters. They say it takes a village, and everyone had some buddies they could call on. Of course, it would start off as a conflict between small groups, but then things would snowball, and eventually you ended up with opposing armies. Anyway, by the time I realized what was happening, there was gang warfare on a daily basis. Folks from the same part of China would stick together, as did people in similar lines of work. In the morning I might give you a piece of my mind, so by evening it was your turn to come looking for me. And just as it started off with some restraint with mostly fists or wrestling, gradually the weapons came out: sticks, iron coal shovels, furnace tongs, the daggers and chain whips young people use for self-defense—some even walked around with chef's knives and metal spatulas. All of it looked pretty intimidating, glinting and gleaming in the moonlight, but when the actual fighting started people mostly played by the rules. Beforehand, the guy at the head of each gang would remind his fighters, "It's not like back home; it's better not to go overboard; everyone's eyes are on us here." So, despite the fact that our neighborhood saw daily action for a while, and a few people did get hurt, everyone kept it under control for the most part. The gang fights were almost a kind of communal entertainment, a salve for dull times. You had to admit there was nothing to get the heart racing like a good brawl, and us shiftless people found it invigorating.

Xingjian and Miluo were big guys, and their repressed aggression had them practically breaking out in acne—they never missed the fun. Before leaving for battle each day, they'd pick over everything in the place that could serve as a weapon. Then they'd head out like Wu Song off to kill the tiger. I was timid by comparison—occasionally I'd join a gang of Jiangxi folk and do some shouting and heckling, but at best I was an instigator. When the real fighting would start, I'm ashamed to say, I'd cower by a wall or under a tree, trembling head to toe. I kept getting migraines—faced with imminent battle I'd be sure to have an attack of nerves, and I could hardly win the struggle against my own head. At times like those, I'd run. Not flee, not escape, but jog. Only those marathon runs soothed my weak nerves.

One evening as Dai Shanchuan drifted, as if sleep-walking, between two armies, I was hiding behind a group of my compatriots. The fighting might spark at any moment, and I heard a kind of glittering sound that slithered into my brain: The migraine was about to start. I slapped my head and said to Xingjian, "It's no good; I need to run."

"Run, then," said Xingjian, holding a scuffed-up baseball bat that belonged to our landlord, his mind already in the fight. "We never expected much from you."

I rapped my temple, drew back like a fleeing soldier, and started running down the moonlit alleyways. When I got to Blossoms Bar, I ran into Dai Shanchuan. Under the light of the moon and streetlamps, he was looking at the display windows and signs of every shop on the street. I stopped to talk to him, and I could hear the mockery in my voice, "Still looking for yourself?"

"Just strolling." He didn't seem to be joking at all. "If there really is another me living in Beijing, I'm going to have to take a good look at the whole city."

We weren't quite on the same frequency. "Haven't you ever considered that your parents were just tricking you?"

"Yeah. But what difference does that make?" He turned his smiling gaze from the shop windows to me. "We all need another self. Imagine if there were another you: Imagine a whole entire life for him. What fun! Since I was a kid, I've wanted to someday get a look at how he lived."

Still not the same frequency. I tried again. "Didn't

you quit school and run away from home to come to Beijing?"

"I told my parents. They said, 'Whatever, go take a look.'"

Okay—the whole family was on their own frequency.

He said, "Has it never occurred to you that there might be another you in the world? Or that you might have a twin brother? And that you and he had accidentally had your names exchanged, and you were here living his life, while he was off somewhere else living yours?"

This was hard to follow. The headache that had receded during my run was starting to return. There might've been something wrong with my head, but this guy was way worse off. "I don't have any brothers, just an older sister."

"But what if you did?" He prompted me earnestly. "Try to remember."

There was no "what if" about it, and I waved him off. Running was the only cure for my nerves; anything else just made me worse. He started speaking again, but I was already on the other side of Blossoms Bar.

*

"But what if you did?" he prompted Duck-egg. "Try to remember. Did your parents say anything?"

Duck-egg put his face in his hands and tilted his head to the side. "They did!" He clapped happily. "My mama said if I kept crying, she'd give all my snacks to my little brother."

"Did your mama say where your little brother was?"

Duck-egg pursed his lips. "No, she just said he looked a lot like me."

He pulled Duck-egg up from the little stool. "Come on, I'll take you to see what your brother looks like."

I stood on the roof, watching Dai Shanchuan leading Duck-egg out of the neighboring courtyard by his little hand.

Duck-egg was four years old, the son of Qiao from Henan. Qiao had no idea what was going on—he, his wife, and Duck-egg had come to Beijing to sell egg crepes, and the parents left early every morning. They pushed their cart to the subway stations or bus terminals and sold the crepes for two-fifty each—three-fifty with an extra egg. They might sell a few hundred crepes per morning, to the young people passing by on their way to work. One of them heated up the crepes they'd made the night before in a frying pan, filling them with crispy-brown fried egg, while the other sold congee and soy milk and made change. The mornings were too early for Duck-egg, so he was stuck at home. Neighbors who didn't need to be out so early would often end up looking after him.

Qiao and his family lived in the courtyard where Dai Shanchuan was renting a place. The difference was, Dai Shanchuan was squeezed into the main room with a bunch of pirated-DVD sellers, while they lived in a standalone room. Western Beijing was full of renters, and anything resembling a house was in hot demand. Lots of landlords put up temporary structures in their courtyards: a single row of stacked brick for the walls, covered up with siding, then topped with asbestos tiles. Enough to keep out wind and rain, but the winters were freezing and summers scorching. Even those cut-rate structures were hot commodities: They were cheap, private, and often relatively clean. Qiao had rented the only one in the courtyard next door.

Duck-egg's name wasn't actually Duck-egg. He had a vaguely duck-egg-shaped head and his parents sold egg crepes, so people called him that. After a while, his parents used the nickname too, and everyone mostly forgot what he'd been called before. Duck-egg was an only child, of that I had no doubt. Qiao had once said it was expensive enough raising one. If they'd had a second, what they'd saved from selling egg crepes wouldn't even cover the fine.

Qiao and his wife left with their cart early in the morning, looking for a safe spot to do business. Even if they had to leave the neighborhood, they hated the thought of a wasted day. Duck-egg was left behind to be entertained by a pack of wastrels. And now Dai Shanchuan had led him away from the courtyard.

They were back twenty minutes later, hardly long enough for me to finish my rooftop nap in the sun. Duck-egg was holding a big photograph, and he called up to me: "Muyu, look! My little brother!"

Little brother? He was an only child. Dai Shanchuan was a real piece of work: He'd taken Duck-egg to a photo shop and found him a little brother. It wasn't a bad picture, though. The photographer had lent him a fashionable little outfit: shirt, tie, and even a little vest with a pocket watch. Dressed up as his brother, hands in his pockets, Duck-egg was quite the sight.

I went to the edge of the roof and said down

to Dai Shanchuan, "Are you trying to screw that kid up?"

"How could I screw him up?" he replied. "Duck-egg is lonely; he spends all day locked up by himself. We need to find him a playmate."

That kind of got to me. When I was young, I got rashes and had to stay out of the wind. My parents were afraid I was infectious and kept me locked up at home, where I got so bored I started talking to the clock and the hot-water bottle. I called down, "Hey Duck-egg, tell me, what's your brother's name?"

"Chicken-egg!" Duck-egg said proudly. "I'm Duck-egg, and my brother's Chicken-egg!"

All right, then. Just don't find him an elder brother, or they'd be chicken, duck, and goose… "Duck-egg, your brother looks a lot like you!"

"Of course," he replied, holding the photo up. "He is my brother."

I had to admit it, Chicken-egg seemed to have the desired effect. It was Dai Shanchuan who told me that Qiao and his wife had expressed their gratitude with two egg crepes, plus a cup of mung-bean porridge. The price of mung-bean porridge was high those days. Some expert had said that eating the beans would cure whatever ailed you, so the supermarkets couldn't keep them stocked, even at triple the price. Qiao said Chicken-egg really did the trick. All he had to do was point to the picture on the wall and Duck-egg would behave, eating, drinking, and sleeping when he was told. He was good when he was left alone, too, talking to the photo—*little brother this, little brother that*—with such enthusiasm that Qiao's wife started talking about having another one.

It all seemed to be true. Qiao and his wife didn't ask me for help watching the boy anymore. Previously, I'd been over there in the mornings every few days, checking to see if Duck-egg had woken up yet.

*

Saturday afternoon there was another big battle, more than thirty per side, all armed—it was quite something to see. Before they got down to business there was a bunch of shouting, as usual. While they were all cursing in each other's faces, a van careened toward them, honking urgently, and everyone leaped back. Someone got knocked down and landed on a hoe. It belonged to a landlord who'd once used it for gardening in a courtyard, but after renting out the space, he left the hoe in a shed, until it was eventually discovered again and pulled out for the fight. To make it more intimidating, the person who found it had polished it so thoroughly you could use it for a mirror, and the sharpness of the edge goes without saying. The wielder happened to be leaning on the handle at the time, so the blade was facing up, and when Fat Cui fell on it, he got it right in the neck, cutting his esophagus and carotid artery. The crowd gathered around to watch him flop like a caught fish, blood and froth pooling around his neck. The burbling sound of his breath coming out but not going in scared everyone half to death, but they could only wring their hands. A couple of the braver ones tried to staunch the blood, while someone called 120. By the time an ambulance showed up, Fat Cui was dead.

I wasn't there that day. Dai Shanchuan had brought Duck-egg up to our roof, and they both had gone on and on about their alter egos. Dai Shanchuan told me that, as he'd passed through the crowd, looking at the astonishing variety of faces, he believed the other Dai Shanchuan who had his face was also searching for him amid the crowd. Thinking about it, he felt connected to the world in innumerable ways—everyone he happened to pass had the potential to be another him. He sensed that he was a knot of vital importance on a vast net.

"Do you really believe there's another you out there?"

"It would be a good thing, wouldn't it?" he said. "Duck-egg really likes his brother now."

"Yeah, I talk to my little brother every day," chimed in Duck-egg, squirming with excitement. "He's a good kid; if you give him candy he won't eat it, but he gives me White Rabbits."

"Congratulations," I said to Dai Shanchuan. "You've found your heir."

Dai Shanchuan grinned at me. Just then Xingjian and Miluo came staggering home. As they passed through the gate Miluo shouted up to the roof, "Cui has passed…"

"Cui who?" I asked.

"Fat Cui!" Xingjian shouted.

"He passed out?" It hadn't occurred to me that Miluo might be capable of euphemism. The only Cui I could think of was the chubby cook from Anhui.

He made a mean fermented perch—he collected the ingredients and cooked in the place he rented. Last time I'd been there, I'd eaten so much I'd nearly swallowed my tongue.

"He's dead!" yelled Xingjian, his voice almost unrecognizable. He'd witnessed the last moments of Cui's life, and it had terrified him.

It seemed unlikely to find your exact double in a crowd. It also seemed unlikely that someone could die at the drop of a hat. Yet Fat Cui was definitely dead. Xingjian and Miluo collapsed in the courtyard, while I slumped on the roof—for a while no one moved. We'd all eaten his fish, drunk his chicken soup. He said there were only three things to know about Anhui cooking: heavy salt, light stink, a bit of thigh. Fat Cui was so modest, he blushed a little when he said, "a bit of thigh."

The thing was, Fat Cui had never had any beef with anyone. He'd just happened to be off work that day. A roommate of his from his hometown who put screen protectors on cell phones for a living had dragged him along to bulk out the crowd.

*

The death shook everyone to their senses. It was dangerous, the game they were playing, and the bigger gangs dispersed without anything else happening. But it was still only the beginning of things. The authorities had been itching to clean up the city and get rid of the ne'er-do-wells here at the outskirts, and now they had their excuse. First it was midnight raids to check residence permits—vagrants without permits were sent back to their villages. Then it was surveys of dangerous or illegal structures in the area—buildings not meeting safety standards couldn't be rented out and would be demolished if not brought up to code in time. Most rentals in the area had something wrong with them, so they were able to dispose of a large batch of the "unstable elements" in the name of safety. Even those with real vendettas had no time to fight: Everyone was busy getting sent back to their hometowns, getting driven out of their rooms, or scrambling for some miraculous reprieve. The rest lit incense in the temples and thanked their good fortune.

As for the three of us, our door was kicked open in the middle of the night and flashlights shone on our pillows. In underpants and a T-shirt, I dug my residence permit out of my suitcase. Miluo couldn't remember where his was and went from box to bag to pockets, finally finding it on a shelf above his bed. He got a kick for his troubles; they said he'd wasted too much time.

While we were looking for our permits, Duck-egg was crying next door. Another squad had gone into Qiao's place, and Duck-egg had been terrified by the strangers barging in in the middle of the night. Qiao must have given them some trouble and pissed them off. As they left, I heard Qiao's wife running out after them, her flip-flops slapping.

"Please don't be angry; that really wasn't what he meant."

"Who cares what he meant!" replied a man's hard voice. "Tell your landlord: day after tomorrow, noon at the latest. No exceptions."

What exactly this referred to I don't know. We didn't get the chance. The neighborhood was in an uproar well before dawn—some packing bags and moving away, others throwing themselves at the mercy of friends and relatives. Over the next two days people were constantly stopping by to say goodbye. Some older migrants who'd been in the city for years said they hadn't seen a sweep that ferocious in years. Then "the day after tomorrow" came and bulldozers roared westward, and we understood the message: enforced demolition of illegal structures. They started in the alleys to the west and worked toward us, house by house. Every building not up to code was knocked down. They knew they couldn't expect the landlords to do it—who would kill their own golden goose? Qiao had called his landlord, but the guy had sworn up and down it was all a bunch of noise, nothing he hadn't dealt with before, no need to get all nervous. But when the bulldozers started down the alleyways, Qiao and his wife lost their nerve and started packing. They hadn't finished yet when the bulldozers came in the gate of their courtyard.

The demolition was a big deal, and we all came out to watch. Dai Shanchuan and the DVD sellers were all there; they had been holed up at home with nothing to do. Dai Shanchuan had nearly gotten himself beaten up during the investigation. He should have been counted as a recently arrived visitor—his train ticket was evidence of that—but while he was explaining his reasons for being in Beijing, he'd pissed off one of the investigators. If I'd been the investigator I would have been furious, too: What the hell did "another self" mean? The little shit was obviously taking the piss, and the policeman's baton was already raised. Luckily Dai Shanchuan realized he wasn't going to be able to explain and just said that he'd come to Beijing to find a brother with whom he'd lost touch years ago. "Why the fuck didn't you just say that to begin with?" the policeman asked. "What was all that bullshit about 'another self'?"

The demolition team leader raised his hand, and the bulldozer approached the eastern wall of Qiao's room. Qiao and his wife said there were still some things inside and asked if they could they have another five minutes. The team leader held up two fingers and glanced at his watch.

Qiao and his wife really panicked. They dashed inside and came out with their arms full of stuff. Dumping everything on the ground, they went back for more; they would have dragged the bed out if they'd had the chance. The team leader dropped his fingers, gesturing to the bulldozer driver, who put his foot on the gas. Duck-egg suddenly started shouting:

"Chicken-egg! Chicken-egg!"

Why was he yelling about eggs? It took me a moment to catch on.

He was crying and yelling, "Chicken-egg! I want my brother Chicken-egg!"

He meant that photo above his bed. I thought of running inside, but the bulldozer was already spouting black smoke and roaring forward. It was Dai

Shanchuan who went in. And less than three seconds later, the bulldozer bit into the wall. The driver hadn't seen him, and by the time he heard us shouting at him over the roar of the engine, it was too late. Qiao's shack shuddered, then collapsed.

The driver sat frozen. We all stood like statues, except for Duck-egg, who was still crying for his brother. Dai Shanchuan did not emerge.

It was a very long moment. Dust rose in the air, and our mouths hung open. We stared at the meager wreckage—asbestos tiles, siding, and bricks all jumbled together. The driver killed the engine, and the courtyard was filled only with the sounds of the wind and Duck-egg's crying. I believe that time has a sound of its own. I could hear that sound, too, as time passed second by second. The pile of wreckage was still. Then another sound suddenly emerged from it, and one of us called out. Through the thinning dust we saw the broken bricks stir, and we could see a hand in the pile, holding a torn and wrinkled photograph above the ruins.

Duck-egg pulled free of his mother, shouting as he ran, "Brother!"

PRINCE
OF MOROCCO

Prince of Morocco

If I hadn't run into that street performer on the subway, I might have gone my whole life never caring where Morocco was. The guy had an amazing voice, sounding like Liu Huan one minute, Chang Yu-sheng the next. After he did Tian Zhen's "At Ease" I started following him—that kind of choked-up, intense, lost-sounding voice could have almost passed for the real singer. Of course, I gave him ten yuan before I started following him. I flushed red when I gave him the money— ten yuan was no small potatoes. But I already had it out, and I couldn't very well put it back away. I had thought for sure I had a single in my pocket, but all three bills I pulled out were tens so, Christ, I gulped hard and gave him one. He thought I was merely enthusiastic and waved to me, saying, "If you like it, follow along and listen." He could tell I was a Tian Zhen fan, and he started singing only her songs: "One Track Mind," "Cheers, Friends," "Crescent-Moon Springs," "Unfinished Love." He sang from one end of the subway train to the other. Then the train reached Xizhimen station, and I had to get off.

He stopped singing and twisted around, pointing

at his back. On his jacket were the words *Prince of Morocco*.

Back in our rooms, I said to Xingjian, "I just met the prince of Morocco... Where's Morocco?"

Xingjian snorted, "Yeah? I met the princess of Spain."

Miluo had already gone to his cabinet of curiosities and fished out a map of the world, which he'd bought for two yuan at a street stall. "North Africa. It's in North Africa. Right underneath Spain. I'm impressed, dude, how'd you know Morocco and Spain were neighbors?"

"My ass, he knew!" I said. Xingjian was always spouting bullshit, but even the accidental win puffed him up a bit. "Gimme that, let's see exactly where this place is."

He spread the map on our little table, and I peered down at it. Morocco was under not only Spain, but Portugal too. To the left was the vast Atlantic, to the right Algeria. To the south it bordered Mauritania, which I'd only ever come across mentioned in a geography book.

We started idly chatting about Morocco. None of us knew a thing about the country besides the name, so we had to make most of it up. We thought up famous mountains and rivers for that abstract bit of territory, along with towers and pavilions and unimaginably large numbers of tourists. As for the prince of Morocco, I said to Xingjian and Miluo, I didn't know if he looked particularly Moroccan, but his nose was pointier than average.

Then we washed up and went to bed, and soon

Morocco and the busker had slipped from our minds. It wasn't that we forgot about it, but all the things that had excited us ultimately had nothing to do with us. Nothing miraculous would ever intrude into our lives. We just lived in these rooms on the western outskirts of Beijing, going about our semi-nocturnal lives. I made my usual rounds of the Line 2 subway, pasting fake-ID ads for my uncle, and Xingjian and Miluo kept on pasting ads for Chen Xingduo; occasionally we'd run into each other in the same alley or subway car. One evening I was eating a baked sweet potato in an out-of-the-wind spot by the Xizhimen station entrance, when Xingjian came up behind me and slapped my shoulder and said, "I saw your prince of Morocco."

"Doesn't that guy have a change of clothes?" said Miluo, behind him. Apparently he'd been wearing the same jacket. "He had a young girl with him, hair like a bird's nest. His little sister?" They'd seen him give the grubby kid a drink of water from his thermos.

How would I know?

"I mentioned you," said Xingjian. "He actually remembered."

I continued working on my sweet potato. You could ignore fully half the things Xingjian said.

"Don't believe it?" Miluo said. "We really did talk about you. We said you gave him ten kuai but that didn't jog his memory; we said you followed him up and down the whole train listening to Tian Zhen songs, and then he knew exactly who we meant. He said, 'Ah, the dude with the yellow Army backpack.'"

I had been carrying a yellow Army backpack that day. Back then I was always carrying that pack—it was the only one I had. All my gear for pasting ads was in there: a big rubber stamp with Thirty Thou Hong's phone number, an ink bottle, an ink roller, business cards with my uncle's number, and pen and paper, just in case. I'd hand out the business cards if I could, use the stamp if necessary, and—as a last resort—write his name and number in pen on any available surface.

"Was that his sister?" Miluo asked again. "She looked a lot worse off than him."

I had no idea. I'd only met the guy once.

I finished my sweet potato and had a cigarette with them. The fall wind kicked up, sweeping leaves and scraps of paper into the subway entrance. A wave of commuters emerged, looking as faint and insubstantial as the autumn twilight. What followed was a snatch of full-throated song. *The white tower reflected on the sea, surrounded by green trees and red walls. Lightly floats the boat on the water, yes, on the water, meeting the cool cool breeze.* There was no guitar, but I knew the prince of Morocco had arrived. Sure enough, out of the subway he came, with a girl with two messy braids. He was teaching her to sing "Raising Our Oars." The girl looked to be six or seven, with a flat nose and dirty face, in a gown made from the flower-printed cloth they use for quilts in the north. The prince looked older than Xingjian and Miluo, maybe early twenties.

"It's you…" said the prince.

"Want a smoke?" Xingjian waved the Zhongnanhai in his left hand.

The prince of Morocco grinned. He pulled a handful of change out of his pocket and handed it to the girl. "Careful crossing the street. Don't forget the lyrics."

The girl hesitated, then took the money and waved goodbye. "Thanks, I'll remember them." She hopped off the curb and headed across the street.

We huddled together, smoking like a pack of juvenile delinquents. I couldn't help myself. "Your sister?"

"Hua? No." The prince was a practiced smoker. "We met on the subway."

"She looks… What does she do?" Miluo asked.

"Puts her hand out."

Which just meant "beggar." There were all kinds of beggars in the subway: cripples, buskers like the prince, old folks, kids like…what had her name been? Hua?

"I kept running into her," the prince said.

"Why did you give her money?" Miluo asked.

"She says if she brings home too little, her ba beats her."

We seethed: What the fuck kind of father was that?! If we got our hands on him, we'd give him a good thrashing.

"Keep your pants on," said the prince. "I wanted to have a word with her old man, too, but Hua wouldn't let me; she was afraid she'd just get beaten worse. What is it you all do?"

I was going to tell him we pasted ads, but Xingjian glared at me. "What's your name?" he asked.

"Wang Feng."

"What's with the 'Prince of Morocco' on your jacket?"

"I always wanted to start a band called 'Prince of Morocco,' with me as the lead singer. I'm working on it. You got another of those smokes?"

So that was it. He was the front man of the imaginary "Prince of Morocco..." the titular "prince." He had the publicity down, anyway. The band was still a complete fantasy, but he already had the name printed on a jacket.

We each had another cigarette. Evening was coming to Xizhimen, and by the time we'd stubbed the butts out, night had fallen.

*

The next afternoon we set out earlier than usual. We got subway tickets and sprawled out on Line 2—as long as you didn't exit a station, you could ride the loop as long as you liked. We went two stops, got off, and waited for the next train, and we kept doing that until we saw Wang Feng. We'd agreed that we were just going to listen to him sing, but we each entertained private fantasies of joining the "Prince of Morocco." To be honest, it was the goal that motivated all three of us. The night before we'd all dreamed of becoming members of the band. Like the bands we saw on TV, in the movies, on the streets, we'd play, we'd sing, we'd jump around. No matter what, being in a band was far more classy than pasting ads for Thirty Thou Hong or Chen Xingduo's fake-ID businesses—that was for sure. But none of us could play an instrument,

nor did we have any idea how to sing, and as for dancing, only Xingjian could manage a bit of half-assed
breakdancing. When we'd gotten back to our place
early the previous morning, Xingjian had sacrificed
his dignity for a while, but when his few moves were
exhausted all he did was repeat the "windshield wiper"—a sort of flopping back and forth that looked kind
of like a windshield wiper. We all wanted to be part
of "Prince of Morocco," but given our lack of skills
we kept quiet and only said we were going to hear
Wang Feng sing. We eventually found Wang Feng
at Yonghegong station, singing Anita Mui's "Flower
Woman." We stood straphanging in a row, and when
Wang Feng's voice faded out on the last line—*women
are flowers, and flowers are a dream*—we applauded
enthusiastically.

"Bravo!"

The subway riders started digging for change. I
gritted my teeth and put my own contribution into
the open mouth of the pleather satchel that hung
from Wang Feng's shoulder; I noted that Xingjian and
Miluo also put in ten yuan each.

Wang Feng continued on to the next car, singing
as he went. He'd start at the first car in the train and
work his way to the last, then get off and wait for the
next one. Then he'd do it all over again. We followed
him, applauding and cheering and occasionally throwing in another coin or two—we really had no money.
In our imaginations, the entire "Prince of Morocco"
band was on tour.

The tour concluded at seven that evening, and
Wang Feng suggested we get something to eat. That

sounded good to us. "Let's see if we can track down Hua," he said. The lead singer had spoken—of course the band would follow. We went looking for her.

We found her at Qianmen station. She was walking slowly through the car, holding a crumpled Master Kong instant noodle bowl. She said nothing, but would bow to the passengers and then gaze beseechingly at them until they gave in and put some money in the container. Only when she was sure there was nothing more coming from a passenger—who was now pretending to be asleep—did she move on to the next and start bowing again.

"Hua!" Wang Feng called out.

Hua caught sight of us and came trotting over to take Wang Feng's hand.

"Have you got enough for today?"

Hua shook her head, pouting pitifully as tears came to her eyes.

"Don't worry, Hua, come eat with us."

The Qianmen restaurant was big enough for only six small tables, but we all thought it was a good spot. How did they make homestyle cooking taste like that? We all drank plenty—except Hua of course; she focused on the food—and we ordered an extra celery and pork strips just for her. Wang Feng could hold his liquor—Xingjian counted up the empties and decided to bow out. If we kept it up, who knew which of us would end up under the table. I figured Wang Feng was the better drinker, because he was still able to pay the bill and then say, quite lucidly, "My brothers came to hear me sing today. No way I'm having them pay for dinner; I'd sell blood twice for that." As we were leaving, he added, "It's settled then: In a few days I'll move in with you all." As we walked out into the night breeze, I realized that half a bottle of beer had gotten me drunk. Wang Feng took Hua's hand and said, "I'll walk you toward home, Hua."

On the way back to our apartment, we decided it had been a most satisfactory and successful gathering. Though we hadn't fully settled the question of the "Prince of Morocco" band, we had inadvertently made Wang Feng one of us. The lease on his basement room was up, and his landlord had increased the rent. He wanted to live someplace with sunlight—he'd had enough of that dark, dank basement. Xingjian had jumped adroitly at the chance, saying with a wave of his hand, "No problem, there's an empty bed at our place, and we'd be honored to have you!" Miluo and I echoed that we'd be honored.

When we got home, Xingjian patted the bed Baolai had vacated. "Once he's here, he's with us."

"Once he's here," Miluo said, "we're with him."

There was nothing to add to such bald declarations, and I just chuckled.

*

Three days passed and it was the weekend. Miluo dug out his almanac and said, nodding sagely, "An auspicious day, suitable for a journey or relocation." There was the sound of a car horn outside: Wang Feng's taxi had arrived.

Besides a guitar that took up some space, Wang Feng had only two pieces of luggage: a suitcase and a woven plastic bag that held a quilt and pillow. When he set some books out by the head of his bed, we discovered he was an honest-to-god music school graduate, though we'd never heard of the school, which seemed to have been a vocational institution. Two of the books were old textbooks, and the rest were biographies or books about film. There was one about Elvis, another about the Backstreet Boys, and still more about the Rolling Stones, the Moyan Trio, and Black Panther. All three of our hearts instantly sank.

We'd planned to move on to the next agenda item after Wang Feng moved in, which was to have a massive "Prince of Morocco" party to celebrate his becoming one of us. Specifically, we'd all head to the courtyard, where Wang Feng would play his guitar and sing, and we'd provide whatever accompaniment or dance moves we could muster. We'd been to the wholesale market by the Beijing Zoo and picked up a cheap tambourine, flute, hulusi, and some cymbals. Miluo had even gotten a suona horn. We couldn't play any of them, but we could learn, right? Wang Feng hadn't been born knowing how to play the guitar or sing. We'd assumed Wang Feng was more-or-less a talented amateur—that he happened to have a good voice and to be good at impressions, so he became a singer. Like any of the performers who gathered from all over in the Beijing subway, all you really needed was guts and a thick skin. But no—he'd gone to school for this. We were suddenly overcome by our own inferiority—none of us had made it through high school.

Even worse were the books about Elvis, the Backstreet Boys, the Rolling Stones, the Moyan Trio, and Black Panther: Every person in them was way too sophisticated for us. Even in torn, beltless jeans, barefoot and bare-chested, they were too sophisticated; you simply couldn't imagine our courtyard producing anyone like them. We could grow our hair out, sure, and strip down to a pair of holey jeans, or even down to our underwear, but we'd never be like them. This reality abruptly sunk our spirits. Xingjian surreptitiously kicked the tambourine under the bed while Wang Feng wasn't looking. Miluo slid the drawer with the hulusi closed. As I was tucking the flute under my blanket, he caught me.

"What's up with you all?" he said. "Did somebody's uncle die?" He yanked my blanket back and snatched the flute. "What's the deal with this?"

I scratched my forehead. "I can't play it."

"But you can learn, right?"

I chuckled; Xingjian and Miluo grinned stupidly, too.

"Something's not right here," Wang Feng said, scanning the room. The place we'd rented wasn't large. Once we'd moved in two bunk beds and a ratty writing desk that doubled as a dining table, there wasn't much space left. He sidestepped some stinky shoes and pulled open the drawer containing the hulusi, which still bore its fake brand label. "Yours?" he asked Miluo.

"I can't play it," said Miluo.

"Neither can I."

Xingjian slapped his neck with a startling smack and said, "Man, we won't beat around the bush. We're hoping we can get in on the fun." He bent down and retrieved the tambourine from under the bed, tossing it to Wang Feng. "You want to start a band, right? Well, we're your guys. We may not know anything about music, but we know how to work like mules."

"It's not about how much you know—we can just put something together for fun," Wang Feng said, sitting and tapping the tambourine against his knee. "Why don't we have a session right now?"

It must have been the oddest performance in history. We went out into the courtyard and propped a broom against a chair for a mic stand, which Wang Feng stood in front of with his guitar. Out of sheer shyness, the three of us insisted on standing in a row behind him, each with an instrument he could only mime at playing. My flute barely touched my lips, Miluo's hulusi hovered somewhere between his nose and forehead, and while Xingjian did beat his drum he did so sporadically, as loud as the spirit took him— nearly inaudibly when his confidence deserted him. But we all gyrated enthusiastically to the rhythm of the guitar. Wang Feng was singing a light-rock version of "My Home Is in the Yellow Earth Hills." Anyone looking through the gate might have thought we were actually insane, bobbing our heads and shrugging our shoulders, thrusting out our chests one moment, our asses the next, and occasionally falling into random fits of twisting and wriggling. By the end of the first song, we were laughing so hard we had to sit down, tears running down our cheeks.

"How was the show?" asked Xingjian.

"A huge success!" said Miluo.

"Teamwork makes the dream work!" said Wang Feng, raising a fist. "Yeah!"

No one said "the band," or "the concert." Nor did we mention the name "Prince of Morocco."

A chill seeped into our backsides from the concrete. Wang Feng was the first to stand. "Up!" he said. "Time is on our side. If you want to learn, I'll teach you. Now that we've got some instruments, we can all learn together."

*

Life went on. The three of us continued our nocturnal ad pasting, while Wang Feng kept taking his guitar down into the subways or into the crowded streets to busk. If we ran into each other, we'd grab a quick meal. Back home, we'd hang out, chatting, boasting, telling dirty stories, and climbing up onto the roof to drink beer, play cards, and gaze out at the swelling city of Beijing—and practice our instruments. I was learning the flute, Miluo the hulusi, and Xingjian both the tambourine and suona. Wang Feng would play his guitar and practice his singing, and he was also learning the instruments he didn't know right along with us. And, of course, we kept gigging, singing, and dancing like the possessed. The sessions often happened in the courtyard, so as not to disturb the neighbors, but when we were happily tipsy we'd climb onto the roof to shout and sing and dance without reserve. As long as we didn't do it at night, the neighbors seemed to enjoy our rooftop shows. Life was typically dull as dishwater, and it wasn't often you saw a bunch of idiots screaming on the roof—they treated us like a spectacle. But no matter what other people thought, music certainly added an unusual savor to our lives. Just thinking about it, I'd feel a pleasing rhythm even in the throbbing veins of my neurotic brain.

Because of Wang Feng, we also ran into the beggar girl Hua more frequently. They had no real connection; Wang Feng saw her often in the subway and felt sorry enough to share his food with her, or his hot water when the weather was cold, and so they'd gotten to know each other. She was a pitiful sight. We all thought poorly of her parents—she should have been in school at her age, but they had her out begging every day in the subway instead. But what could we do? She was their kid, and there was no point in calling the police—they couldn't spend all their time watching out for her. There were a lot of kids like her, scattered throughout every corner of the city, asking passersby for money, bowing to everyone, faking disabilities, carrying little speakers to play music or warbling tuneless songs. Not long ago the news had reported about a university professor encountering a couple begging with their eight-year-old son, and when he scolded them for not sending their kid to school, they replied, "Where would we get the money for school?"

"You can earn it." The professor had responded.

"What do you think we're doing?!"

Following a bit more back and forth, the parents had said, "If you're so high-minded, if you've got a real sense of duty, why don't you pay for his schooling?"

The crowd had burst into laughter and the professor slunk away.

What I simply couldn't accept was that Hua's parents were actually setting a quota for her each day: 50 yuan today, 55 tomorrow, 60 the day after... One day Wang Feng came back after a day of busking swearing all over the place, calling Hua's parents animals—they'd raised Hua's quota nearly to 100. If she couldn't make it, she'd likely get a hiding.

Back then, 100 yuan per day was no small amount.

"There's nothing to it," said Xingjian. "First thing is we go put the sticks to those bastards."

"After a good beating," said Miluo, "we'll see if they dare touch a hair on Hua's head!"

"The problem," said Wang Feng, lighting a cigarette, "is that Hua refuses to take me to see her parents. It's also my fault—I give her money sometimes, and it whetted their appetite. Now they're going to kill the goose—they keep setting her goal higher."

It really was his fault, in a sense. The first time he'd seen Hua her bowl was mostly empty and she was crying in the subway entrance, so he'd given her fifteen yuan. The second time he saw her crying, he gave her twenty. The third time she was too terrified to go home, and he gave her another twenty. A boat rises with the tide, but in this case the only things rising were Hua's parents' demands. They felt certain she could earn more, so they upped the quota. His good deeds meant that Hua was even more terrified of going home than before. And Wang Feng couldn't keep helping her fill a pit that constantly grew deeper.

"Wang Feng, don't try to think your way out of

this," said Xingjian, propping a foot up on the chair. "Let's do it my way: with a tune-up. Give them a solid message."

"But we can't even get near them."

Miluo propped his foot on the chair, too. "Let's follow the breadcrumbs."

The next evening, well rested and full of donkey burgers, we got a text from Wang Feng: *7 PM, Fuxingmen station.* There wouldn't be much thrill in following her; she was just a kid. In the course of our work, we had to watch out for the cops, so we'd learned the basics of tailing and losing tails. After a couple of bus transfers, we sauntered over to the subway station; Wang Feng and Hua were there waving goodbye to each other, one heading east, the other west. Miluo pulled up the hood of his sweatshirt and followed her, head down. Xingjian came along twenty meters behind him, then me, and finally Wang Feng.

The route was complicated, and we weren't quite sure where we ended up. A left turn, a right turn, with traffic, against traffic, across a pedestrian bridge—Hua walked hesitantly, as if something were on her mind, and she kept throwing glances behind her. I held up and asked Wang Feng if we'd given the game away, but he said no. He'd had to hurry Hua along in order to have her leave the station at the agreed-upon time, and so he'd ended up giving her thirty yuan. "I've got almost nothing left," said Wang Feng.

"You've escorted her home before, so you must have some clue?"

"A clue, barely," he said. "We got to the Fuxingmen station, I turned to light a cigarette, and she was gone."

Hua stopped and sat down on the curb, arms around her knees. There was a streetlight overhead, and her shadow was huddled under her body. We approached slowly—there was a constant flow of pedestrians and cars, movement everywhere, so we were unlikely to be noticed. Suddenly she stood and darted straight out into the road; a car slammed on its brakes, the screeching sound piercing my brain. Hua must have been stunned: She stood stock-still, the bumper of the Audi A6 only millimeters from her. Wang Feng broke into a run, and I followed. Hua still hadn't moved, and only when Wang Feng scooped her up her whole body did it begin to tremble. The driver got out of his car, clearly in a cold sweat and flustered.

"Is this kid trying to kill herself? And you all— can't you keep an eye on her?! I've got OCD, okay? How am I supposed to drive now?"

Wang Feng apologized and carried Hua to the sidewalk. She clung to him as she finally started to cry. In the streetlight, the corner of her eye and the back of her right hand looked purplish. Xingjian and Miluo also gathered around.

"They'll beat me!" Hua said through her sobs. "They'll beat me to death!"

I leaned over to Xingjian. "I wonder if they aren't her real parents."

Xingjian slapped his neck. "Huh, why didn't I think of that?"

The first order of business was getting Hua home. But she wouldn't let us take her, wouldn't even let us watch her leave—she insisted we go first. She said we were already too close to her home.

The mission was aborted; we did as she asked. On the way we talked about the possibility that she wasn't staying with her biological parents, and Wang Feng said he'd had the same thought. When Hua spoke of her parents, she always referred to "them" or "they." What kind of parents were called "them" by their kid?

*

A few days later, Wang Feng came with proof, and our suspicions were confirmed. At his urging, Hua had finally admitted the truth: Her "parents" had eight children between the ages of five and fourteen, and except for the youngest boy—whom his "parents" took with them to beg in bus stations and places like that—the kids all operated alone. They left early and stayed out late, staking out their own spots, each with a daily quota of between fifty and a hundred yuan. The whole "family" lived in a two-room apartment not far from Fuxingmen, and Hua slept with three "sisters" on a mattress on the floor. She could find the apartment with her eyes closed but didn't know what the neighborhood was called—she couldn't read, and her "parents" weren't about to send her to school.

"Are any of the kids theirs?"

"An eleven-year-old girl and the youngest boy," said Wang Feng. "None of the others."

"Was Hua…trafficked?" I said hesitantly. The papers were reporting stuff like that every day, but it still seemed weirdly distant.

"Bought and sold a few times."

Which was to say, not even Hua knew how she'd ended up with her "parents" or how she came to be in Beijing. She was five years old when she was taken from her home.

"How old is she now?"

"Ten."

She was on the small side. But no surprise, after years of living in fear and eating poorly. She was probably malnourished.

"How much does she remember about her past?"

"Not much. Just that her real father stank of alcohol, and she thinks she had a brother."

"Where's she from?"

"Dunno. She remembers being on a mountain with her dad. He was slumped against a rock by the side of the road, reeking, when someone came along with a lollipop and lured her away."

"What then?"

"After that she ended up in a bunch of different places, with different people. Sometimes she was given decent food, sometimes she was beaten and given nothing."

"What was the name of the mountain?"

"She can't remember. Wang Feng had told her to think back and try."

One afternoon a couple days later, while we were all sleeping, Xingjian's phone beeped. It was a text from Wang Feng: *Longhu Mountain. Can you find that?* Hua had managed to remember the name; she thought the mountain was close to her home.

We jumped out of bed and went straight for

Haidian Book City. The three of us split up and started searching the bookstore. Xingjian went for the historical sites and scenic spots, Miluo for famous mountains and great rivers, and I took maps. At a quarter to eight that evening, I found Longhu Mountain on a map of Jiangxi Province. At the bottom-left corner of the map was a note: "Longhu Mountain is located within the bounds of Guixi county township, twenty kilometers southwest of Yingtan." We each looked up anything else we could find about Longhu Mountain, including its geographical surroundings, local customs and culture, and local cuisine. We tried to gather everything and anything that might trigger Hua's memories. When we got back home, Wang Feng was already there, and we dumped out all the information we'd gathered. Wang Feng thought about it and said there might be something Jiangxi-flavored in Hua's otherwise unplaceable Mandarin accent.

After a bit more research we were fairly certain that Hua's home was somewhere near Yingtan, in Jiangxi. Wang Feng tried bringing up some of the more characteristic elements of Yingtan daily life, and some images began to surface from the depths of Hua's memory. She was anxious, and with each new bit of information she divulged, she insisted that Wang Feng keep it quiet, in case her Beijing "parents" find out. She wanted to leave them, but at the same time was afraid—to her, the world was primarily a place of danger. The four of us continued our daily discussions of how to help her contact her real parents, but no matter how we wracked our brains we couldn't think of where to start. She had no memory of her parents' names or the village where they lived; she didn't even remember her own family name. We talked about it constantly, but every day ended in frustration.

One Thursday afternoon, Wang Feng came home only two hours after he'd gone out, trailing Hua, who was eating a McDonald's hamburger. She had a cut at the corner of her mouth and was chewing carefully, despite clearly being starving. Her cheek and left wrist were bruised, and she was walking with a limp: Her knee was hurt. Her "dad" had beaten her the night before. She'd brought in quite a bit during the day, and when she got home her "parents" weren't back yet. She lay down on the mattress and fell asleep, but when she woke thirty yuan was missing from her pocket. Her brothers and sisters all just shook their heads, and her "father" exploded, giving her a sound thrashing.

"She can't go on like this," said Xingjian.

"Step one is still beating the crap out of him," said Miluo.

"She should be with her family," I said.

Wang Feng bummed a smoke from Xingjian and drew on it like he was trying to kill it. "Maybe..." he said, "we could take her back to Yingtan?"

Wang Feng spoke very slowly; I guessed he was a little spooked by his own idea. He didn't mean just put her on a bus—he meant go with her to find her parents. A needle-in-a-haystack situation. The room went quiet; the only sound was Hua chewing small mouthfuls of hamburger.

"Hua, do you want to go back to your real home?" asked Wang Feng.

She was unsure, too, looking at each of us in turn, then saying fearfully, "I don't know."

"Don't be afraid, Hua, you can tell me." Wang Feng brought her a cup of water. "Do you want to go home?"

"Ma… Ba… I really don't know." Hua began to cry.

"Hua, if you want to go home, just nod and I'll take you there. I'll help you find your parents."

We all watched her. She put down her hamburger, and after a full minute, she nodded her head.

"All right, let's go buy some train tickets!"

*

"So, we're sure?"

"We're sure."

Xingjian, Miluo, and I each pulled out 200 yuan to give Wang Feng, to show our support. It was the best we could do. Wang Feng told us not to worry; he'd be back within a month for sure. If necessary, he could always perform while they searched, and maybe Hua could sing with him. She'd learned a bunch of songs over the past few weeks and was sounding pretty good. We had our goodbye dinner on the roof, with beer and donkey burgers.

I began keeping a tally with 正 characters on the courtyard wall: one stroke per day, five strokes per character. A week passed. Two weeks passed. A month. Forty days. Wang Feng sent a text saying they were still searching; Yingtan was bigger than he'd thought. The good news was that Hua's singing was continuing to improve and she'd started to learn the guitar—she was a natural.

Two months passed. It was mid-winter in Beijing.

The day before the fourteenth 正 was complete, heavy snows fell on Beijing, and Xingjian, Miluo, and I huddled in our room, eating hotpot. We'd borrowed the pot and were boiling three heads of cabbage and three kilograms of pork belly. Engulfed in steam, we got a phone call from Wang Feng. It must have been freezing in Yingtan—Wang Feng was practically shouting; we didn't even need to put him on speakerphone.

"Xingjian, Miluo, Muyu: You guys have got to vouch for me, tell them I was bringing Hua home..."

The wind was loud in Yingtan, but the voices were louder. A rough male Jiangxi voice burst through Xingjian's phone: "Vouch for you? Who the hell would believe that?"

Another angry voice followed: "To hell with this bullsh—"

We heard an even stronger wind, then a sudden smash. Then nothing but the insistent, endless busy signal. Xingjian shouted, "Hello! Hello!" into the phone for a while, then hung up and called again, only to get a gentle woman's voice:

"The number you have dialed is not in service. Please check the number and try again."

*

Three months later, after the New Year, we joined the vast swells of people returning from their hometowns to Beijing. Beijing was once again that sprawling, borderless, teeming metropolis. One afternoon I came home from picking up some freshly printed ads from Thirty Thou Hong to find a young girl in a pink-and-white parka sitting on our doorstep. I coughed and she looked up—it was Hua.

"Hua! Where's Wang Feng?"

"He hasn't come back yet?"

"Did you ever find your Ma and Ba?"

"We did." She kicked at the threshold for a while. "But then my ba said it was Wang Feng who'd kidnapped me."

Holy shit. It had precisely nothing to do with Wang Feng! But Hua's father had sunk his teeth in, saying to a crowd that had gathered: "Look, she's going around busking with this guy, and of course all the earnings go to him. Just listen to my daughter's singing! You heard her, right? A girl her age would have to study for years to learn that many songs and sing them so well. You think he was just bringing her home? My ass! You believe there are good people out there? No, you don't, do you? Let's take that instrument of his and his money. A guy like that belongs in jail! Look at him, the fat, satisfied bastard, never done a real day's work, and dares to bully my poor girl practically at her own door!"

They'd smashed his phone and taken him to the police. Neither his nor Hua's explanations did any good. When Wang Feng explained, they wouldn't listen. When Hua explained, they said she was saying it out of fear of reprisal. There in the village, the whole thing suddenly became perfectly simple: What they said was how it was. That's how it had to be. There wasn't anything else to say.

That was the last time Hua had seen Wang Feng.

I opened the gate, but Hua wouldn't come in. She said, "I just came to see you all." Suddenly she started crying. "I thought he'd be back."

He didn't come back.

A few days later, Xingjian and Miluo said they'd seen Hua on the subway. She had a guitar and she sang pretty well. She was followed by a short man, who was collecting the money.

"Guess who the guy was?" Miluo asked me.

"Hua's real father."

"How'd you know that?

I'd guessed.

"They look goddamn exactly alike," said Xingjian. "The same nose."

THE DOG'S BEEN
BARKING
ALL DAY

The Dog's Been Barking All Day

Patching up the heavens was something only Chuan
would think of trying. He stood on our roof—hammer
in his left hand, nail in his right—banging at the sky.
A cloud came over: "I nailed it." A plane flew past:
"I nailed that, too." Zhang Dachuan and his wife,
Li Xiaohong, said, "Look how clever our son is: He
knows a needle and thread would never do it. You need
a hammer and nails to patch up the heavens." They
were in the courtyard, looking upward. Under a rare
blue Beijing sky, their eight-year-old son, Chuan, held
his hammer and nail high, looking for all the world
like a heroic giant. From where they stood, I towered
just as tall: I was on the roof next to him, hovering over
Chuan to keep him safe.

Chuan was wrong in the head. His parents were
fruit sellers, and they spent all day every day in the cab
of a three-wheeled flatbed, selling piles of apples in
apple season, oranges in orange season, watermelons
in watermelon season. On occasion they had bananas,
mandarin oranges, pineapples, or pears. Cherries were
the most expensive. Xiaohong couldn't understand
why city people were crazy for the tiny, overpriced

things, which they insisted on calling by their English name, *che-li-zi*. Chuan was happiest following me around. When I wasn't out pasting ads, Dachuan and Xiaohong would lead him over to our yard, bringing apples and oranges with them: "Chuan, you play with your brother Muyu." They'd bring his lunch in a box, of course, and I'd warm it up for him at noon. If Xingjian and Miluo were around, they would give us extra apples and oranges. Then their three-wheeler would start its rattling roar, and they'd call out to Chuan, who stood, cocked-headed and drooling, with his hammer and his nail in a sack:

"Be good! Say bye-bye to mommy and daddy."

This isn't about Chuan, or Zhang Dachuan, or Li Xiaohong. Much less is it about that three-wheeler that went puttering from dawn to dusk through the streets and alleys of Beijing, piled with fruit. This is about a dog, the one that Dachuan and Xiaohong kept to guard the courtyard and two-room building they rented next door to ours. They lived in one room and kept their fruit in the other. The dog was tied outside the fruit room to keep thieves and children away. We hated that dog. It started barking every morning as soon as the three-wheeler started rattling. As the three-wheeler pulled away, it continued barking. As the three-wheeler trundling through Beijing's alleys all day, it never stopped barking.

"Someday that fucking dog is going to get it," my roommates said.

The dog woke early, which meant no rest for us. Our jobs pasting ads around the city meant we were more-or-less nocturnal and were usually crawling into bed around dawn, right as the little shit started up. Even if we weren't out the night before we might take a nap at noon, and that thing could have you awake and sweating at the ankles with a single yap. Someday that fucker was going to get it.

We hadn't gone out that day. After lunch I took Chuan up to the roof to fix the sky. Xingjian was poring over Prince Gong's *Interpretation of Dreams*—he'd had a dream that a white hog with peach flowers on its face was knocking on our door, and when he opened it, he'd woken up. Miluo was inserting line breaks into a paragraph he'd written the night before—he thought he might have the potential for poetry. They wanted an afternoon nap, but it was impossible: The dog just kept barking. And barking, and barking. And barking. Who knew why it had gone haywire. From the roof I could hear the two of them cussing and bitching. The earth-shattering rattle of the three-wheeler became audible, approaching from a distance, and Chuan raised that same damn hammer and that same damn nail and said, "My ba! My ma! Look, my ma and ba!"

His parents were back.

Xingjian and Miluo came out of our room and called up to me, "Tell them to take their rugrat back!"

"I'm playing with him," I said. "No skin off your nose."

"Hell with that," Xingjian said. "That dog is driving me nuts!"

"Not only do we have to listen to their dog," added Miluo, "we have to help them raise their idiot. It's not right! Send him home."

The three-wheeler stopped outside the courtyard, and Chuan's parents got out, all smiles. They'd sold a whole load of oranges that morning, and they were planning on restocking and doing it again.

"Are you having fun playing, son?" asked Dachuan.

Xiaohong added, "Remember to treat Muyu with respect."

I had to lie and say I was going to my uncle's place to pick up a fresh batch of ads. Thirty Thou Hong was really keeping up with the times, I told them; had they ever heard of a fake-ID peddler with business cards? Anyway, I'd have to return Chuan to them.

They seemed a little unhappy, but made sure to keep up their smiles. The kid *was* theirs, after all. The dog was still barking. I passed Chuan down to Li Xiaohong, who pursed her lips and asked for the lunchbox, too. "Did you do something to annoy them?" she asked Chuan under her breath. Chuan twisted his head and body around to look at me, stuck out his tongue, and grinned.

"Big brother likes me."

His eyes never seemed to focus on the same spot. It drove me nuts; I always felt he was looking at someone else when he was talking to me. But he was right—I did like him. He always said what he was thinking, or what he wanted to do—he hadn't learned hypocrisy. His ba could have taken a lesson from him. Dachuan was always going on about how much they loved their son, how they couldn't bring themselves to have another, even though government policy allowed for a second child if the first was disabled. "But if we had another," said Dachuan, all smiles, "little Chuan wouldn't be happy." He took Chuan from Xiaohong, holding him by the armpits, and heaved him into the three-wheeler's cab. Chuan's head smacked audibly against the cab's back divider. Dachuan's face twitched, and he hissed under his breath:

"No crying!"

The three-wheeler passed through the gate, restocked with oranges, apples, and bananas, and rattled away. Chuan was next to his father, and Xiaohong was in the back, on top of a heap of apples. The dog barked with greater abandon.

The two of them were from the countryside, but they'd traveled all over and their accents had wandered with them. You couldn't tell, exactly, what kind of accent they had. Dachuan was always adding the Beijing *arrr* sound to the end of all his words: *They wurrr lining up for the apprrrs and orangerrrs.* It infuriated Xingjian: "Where the fuck does he get *orrrf*, with his '*wurrs*' and his '*apprrrs*'?"

He transferred his irritation about Dachuan's accent to their family dog.

"It's *still* fucking barking!" he said. "I'm going to kill that little mutt! It would be one thing if it were a German shepherd, but it's not even a Pekingese; it's just a filthy mutt. I'm going to kill the little shit!"

No sooner had he said it than he and Miluo were out of the door, both of them in a rage. It wasn't just the fact that their nap had been interrupted. I suspected that Prince Gong's interpretations were turning out bogus, and Miluo's line-breaking career wasn't panning out. But they couldn't simply kill the animal—it would be obvious who'd done it—so they decided just to mess with it for a while. Miluo was holding a bowl of leftover pork-rib stew, the broth half congealed in the cold.

"You stay up on the roof," Xingjian directed me. "Tell us the second you hear them coming back."

I grabbed an old copy of *The Arabian Nights* I'd found in a book stall and crawled back up on the roof. There's no better place to read than on a roof. The buildings in western Beijing are low to the ground; life there was held low to the ground, too. From my elevated seat I felt I could see the whole world clearly. Even a book made more sense up there than it would in any classroom. I sat down near the edge bordering the alley. The dog barked even more wildly as the two of them climbed over the wall. Miluo fished a bone from his bowl of broth and tossed it to the dog, which snuffled at it and immediately stopped barking.

Truly, there was nothing remarkable about the dog, it was just a black and white mutt, so filthy from rolling in the dirt and its own muck that there wasn't much difference between the black and the white. It lived outdoors in a crude doghouse and was so accustomed to being cold that it curled up into a ball any time it sat down. I doubted whether it had ever eaten its fill: Its curved ribs seemed about to poke through its hide. The dog's name was "dog." That's what Dachuan and Xiaohong called it: "Come here, dog! Quit barking, dog! Fuck off and die, dog!" Now it was lying with the bone between its front paws, almost too excited to gnaw it. Xingjian and Miluo dragged two folding stools from the corner of the yard and sat down to watch the dog, which trembled as it chewed. Xingjian looked back at me and snapped his fingers. The afternoon sunlight was weakening, and the dog's shadow inched out into a blob.

"We're giving him a taste," Miluo said to me.

The Arabian Nights is a good book. Up on the roof, it was an even better book. It brought me instantly out of my low-to-the-ground life. I flipped through it randomly, reading bits here and there.

The dog still hadn't managed to crunch up and swallow the bone—in its exertion it was wheezing like an asthmatic. But it wouldn't give up and kept biting the bone, then spitting it out, then biting it again. Xingjian stuck his finger in the congealed broth then brought it to his nose, his eyes closing in pleasure as he smelled it. The dog seemed to understand his expression: It suddenly went quiet, then came over and lay docilely at his feet. Xingjian raised his chin and made a sign at Miluo, who came over and gave the dog a kick. The dog had no idea what was happening. It leaped up, gave a single bark, then went quiet and lay back down. Miluo gave it another kick, and it leaped up again, looking back at him, its bark becoming a drawn-out growl that trailed off strangely. It hesitated for a few seconds, then lay down again. Miluo looked at Xingjian, who grinned and nodded, and a third kick landed on the dog's belly. This time it really did get angry; it jumped up and spun around several times, as Xingjian and Miluo instinctively scooted their stools back. They were in no danger, though: The dog was already at the limit of its chain. It barked, but they no longer found the barking annoying. They looked up at me and grinned.

"Want to come down?" asked Miluo.

"What are you going to do?"

"Don't worry, we're just playing with the little fucker," Miluo answered, landing another kick on the dog's haunches.

The dog was really going nuts, yanking at its chain so that it clanked and jangled. Xingjian quickly scooped out another blob of congealed broth and flicked it on the ground, and the dog went after it. It licked the whole patch of ground. It must have been delicious. Afterward it slowly lay down again—smacking its mouth—put its head on its front paws, and started barking again. There was a note of pleading and of sorrow in its barks. Xingjian passed the bowl to Miluo and moved his stool close to the dog, then began petting it as if it was his own dog, working through its fur from its head, down its back to its tail. The dog closed its eyes. From where I was sitting, it looked as though Xingjian was planning to give it a punch in the head, but the moment he made a fist he relaxed his hand again—perhaps seeing that the dog's tail was wagging furiously. He continued rubbing it, starting again at the head and moving over its emaciated back to its bony haunches to its tail, smoothing the fur from base to tip. He stood up.

"Take a look to see if they're coming back, will you?" He said to me.

I stood up, my faint shadow stretching broad and long over the roof, all the way to the far side. On days like today the sun was weak as a sick man, strength exhausted by a few sneezes. In the distance were ping-fangs; in the greater distance were more pingfangs and a few trees with bare branches like pencil sketches on the horizon, and the occasional taller building. The sun seemed ready at any moment to drop on those buildings and those trees. I looked up the alley and saw nothing, not even a pedestrian, as if the western suburbs of Beijing had suddenly emptied. I waved a hand at them.

"Quit reading that stupid book," said Xingjian. "It won't bring you any fairy tales, not in this life or the next. I've got something to show you."

He gestured to Miluo and took the bowl back. This was Miluo's job—he dipped his hand in the bowl and came up with a handful of congealed broth, which he smeared on the dog's tail. The dog caught the scent and began barking excitedly.

"Still fucking barking!" Xingjian gave it a kick.

The dog stifled its barks and twisted in search of the scent. The broth did smell good—I caught a whiff of it from the rooftop. A plane passed overhead: one of Chuan's patches. If you didn't see Chuan's perpetually unfocused eyes, his strangely cocked head, and his endless string of drool, you wouldn't know anything was wrong with him at all. He had more imagination in him than most people, more than in *The Arabian Nights*— who would have thought of patching the sky? Who could have understood that needle and thread wouldn't do it, that you needed a hammer and nails?

The dog was spinning in circles after its own tail. The chain slowly wrapped around its legs; it didn't know to step over it. It managed a few licks to the tip of its tail, which made it all the more frantic to get another taste.

Everyone's seen a dog chase its tail, but we'd never witnessed such a clumsy, frenzied, disorderly pursuit. We started laughing. It was grunting and yelping as it attempted to lick its own tail, barking when it couldn't reach it. Eventually it discovered that if it twisted its body violently it could just reach the tip, and soon had licked it clean.

Xingjian and Miluo talked quietly. Clearly, putting more broth on the dog's tail was tantamount to simply feeding it directly, and where was the fun in that? Soon they reached a consensus: They'd add more broth bit by bit, higher and higher up the tail. How high could he reach?

This made things difficult for the dog: It needed to bend itself practically in half, and by the end it simply couldn't manage. The chain wasn't making things any easier, tripping and tangling it, and it finally fell in a heap, so frustrated that it bit the chain and began shaking it back and forth. Xingjian and Miluo only stood nearby and laughed. I had to admit, it was a rare bit of fun. I stood up on the roof and shouted:

"Take the chain off!"

They liked that idea. Xingjian flicked a little broth on the ground, and while the dog was busy with it, Miluo undid its collar. A new round of tail-chasing ensued. The removal of the collar and chain didn't actually give the dog much more freedom of movement, but it was certainly an encouragement, and the dog strove all the harder to bite its tail. I don't know what sounds a person in complete despair might make, but as the dog failed to lick the base of its tail it made a sound of boiling rage that for a moment sounded almost human. The sound caused a chill to run through me, as though it were ice water and not the chill breeze of dusk passing over me. The game seemed to have gone far enough.

The breeze brought the sound of a diesel engine. I cocked an ear, but it seemed to disappear. But…there it was again. It was time to remind Xingjian and Miluo that enough was enough. They were watching the dog twisting itself up like a potato bug, doubled over themselves with laughter. The dog gave a last desperate yelp, folded itself, and sank its teeth into its own tail. In pain and shock, it levitated straight into the air, body still locked in a circle, and seemed to hang there for a couple of seconds before it smacked down with a seemingly audible crack of bone on ground. It let go of its tail, yelping all the more piteously, and made straight for the gate of the yard.

It was an old-style courtyard with an iron gate whose two halves were chained shut. It was large enough to admit the three-wheeler directly into the yard. The gap between the locked halves was wide, but not wide enough to let a dog squeeze out, no matter how skinny. That day, however, it was crazed enough to try, though it succeeded only in ramming into one half of the gate. It made one more turn, circling into the far corner of the yard to get a running start, and this time went for the stump of a long-dead cedar tree next to the courtyard wall. It leaped onto the stump, then successfully scrabbled up and over the wall, landing on the road outside with another solid smack of bone and flesh on concrete.

"Get out!" I yelled. "They're back!"

The sound of the diesel engine had already entered the alleyway. It was Zhang Dachuan's three-wheeler, no mistake. Still shocked by the dog's escape, Xingjian and Miluo stood open-mouthed for a moment before vaulting the wall themselves.

The dog had struggled up and taken off running with an unsteady gait. It staggered like a drunk but was going fast. The three-wheeler had just turned into the alleyway and was approaching at a jaunty speed—the fruit had sold well again; the back was empty. The dog headed straight for it, as if welcoming long-lost relatives, and Dachuan was obviously surprised—he didn't swerve until the last minute. As he did, he hit the brakes hard and the three-wheeler flipped. The cries of dog, man, and woman rose from the alley.

By the time I'd gotten down from the roof and run over there, the front wheel of the three-wheeler had stopped spinning. The dog was splayed on the ground to the side, still barking. Xiaohong knelt in front of the three-wheeler, weeping as she tried to get into the cab, the door yawned open to the darkening sky. On the other side, Chuan had ended up—God knows how—jammed in the door, his upper body inside the cab, his lower body outside it, crushed between the cab and the ground. The weight of the unloaded three-wheeler bore down on him, and dark blood was winding out across the pavement.

Xiaohong cried for Chuan, her voice already hoarse. He didn't respond. Not the slightest sound. Dachuan had gotten one shoulder under the cab of the three-wheeler and was trying to heave it back upright. I set my shoulder next to his. The dog was still barking, sounding nothing like a dog.

Night was falling. Two figures approached, as unsteady as the dog: Xingjian and Miluo. They joined us in righting the three-wheeler. I heard Dachuan's flustered, urgent voice.

"Stop your crying, Xiaohong, all right? Now we can have another! One that's right in the head and right in his body. And you won't have to feel sorry for him. And you won't have to worry we won't be able to raise him. Just stop your crying, won't you!"

A couple of weeks later, rummaging through a book stall, I found in a book that one of the uses of a dog's tail was to help it keep balance. "When running fast or accelerating, a dog's tail will stretch out straight behind it; when turning corners it will swing back and forth; when slowing down it rotates in a circle, similar to a parachute deployed behind a swiftly decelerating aircraft." As far as I could remember, when Dachuan's dog ran, its tail drooped like a broken feather duster.